PAM KOWOLSKI IS A MONSTER!

SARAH LANGAN

RAW DOG SCREAMING PRESS

Pam Kowolski is a Monster © 2025 by Sarah Langan

Published by Raw Dog Screaming Press
Bowie, MD

First Edition

Printed in the United States of America

This is a work of fiction. Any resemblance to persons living or dead is unintentional.

ISBN: 978-1-947879-89-8 / 978-1-947879-91-1
Library of Congress Control Number: 2025933103

RawDogScreaming.com

Also by Sarah Langan

A Better World
Good Neighbors
Audrey's Door
The Missing
The Keeper

for Mary Brennan Magee

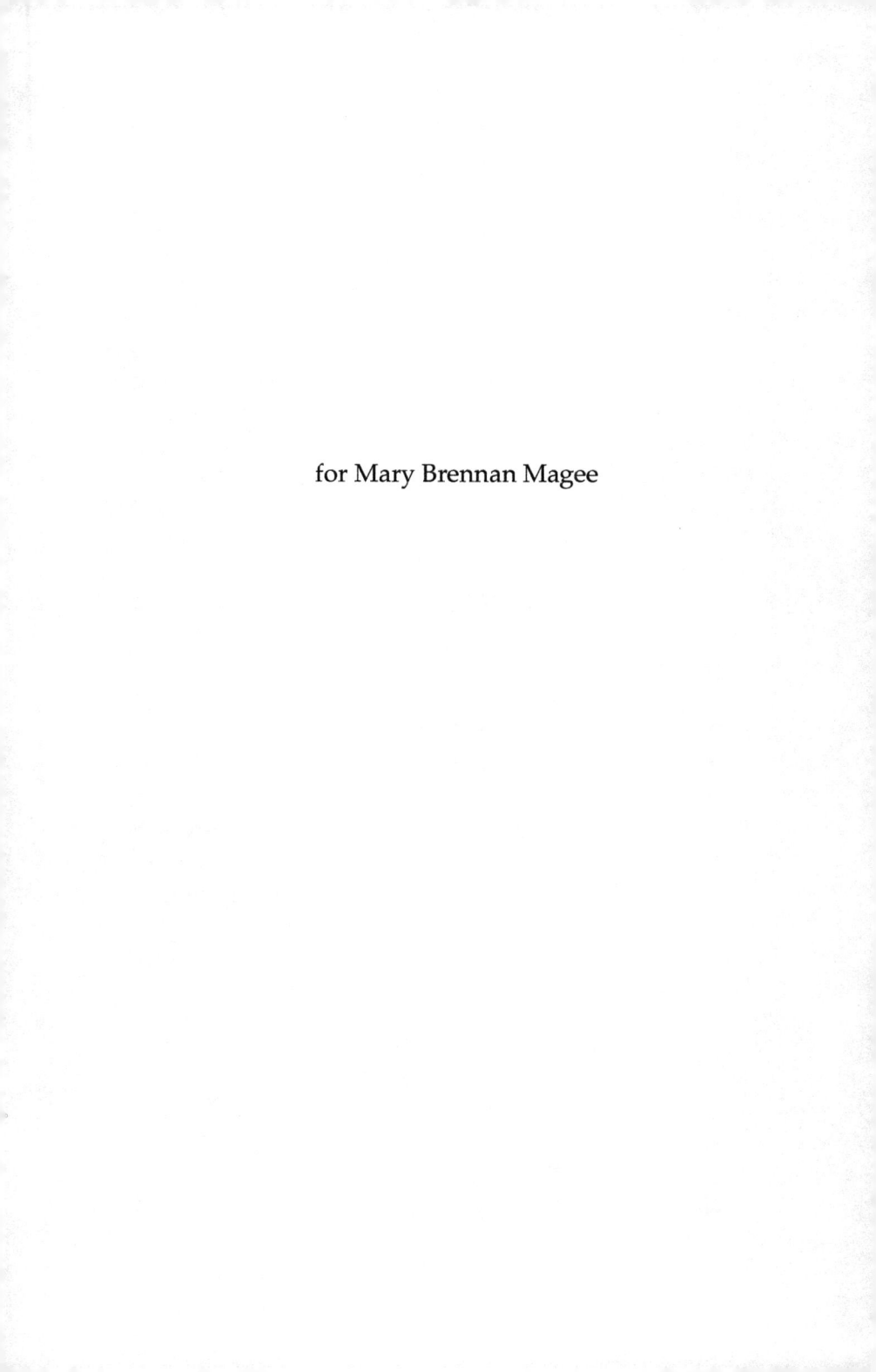

Scripple-scrapple.

The night Madam Pamela's Big Reveal went catastrophically wrong, I was staying in her guesthouse, waiting for the interview that I hoped would revive my career. From the window, I watched her staff flee. Wide-eyed and terrified, they raced, shocked too insensate to scream. Little whirls of gravel dust cycloned up from the circular driveway as their fancy electric cars peeled out. Some didn't bother with cars. In dressy-casual business slacks, they ran.

The mansion glowed with a kind of phosphorescence. Inside was *Pam's Parlor of Extraordinary Delights*, from which she broadcast her hit psychic show *The Madam Pamela Hour*. She'd built Split Foot Mansion here in Detroit because she claimed that this specific location was the most magic on earth, where meridians intersected, opening a gateway between worlds. With the aid of her "spirit companion" she'd dug a hole through the floor of her *Parlor*, where she claimed she'd broken the barrier between the visible and the unknown.

Glory Hole, I'd joked in a blog.

Right now, she was broadcasting her Big Reveal. For $200 per view, people were supposed to learn Madam Pamela's secrets. She'd promised to let them see the world from her eyes. What was it she saw? She'd told us explicitly—dreadful drearies, she called them. Until lately, I'd assumed she was lying.

Pam Kowolski was rich, famous, and successful. I'd hated her for a long time. When I'd learned about her Big Reveal, I'd spent months researching this story, in the hopes of writing the pitch-perfect hit piece to take her down. I'd fantasized about her destruction, her *hurt* at my hands. How stupid. How blind.

I came out from the guest house. In the settled, pregnant stillness, a sound emanated from the mansion: *scripple-scrapple*. Something dreadful come round at last.

For me, there wasn't a choice. There never had been. The staff had left Split Foot's door wide open. I walked through.

It was time for our interview.

Crime Scene

I discovered Pam Kowolski on a late winter night. She practically apparated across my screen, her hair like black gloss, her smile a gash of red lipstick.

My apartment was the top floor of an Astoria, Queens walk-up. The landlord lived right below and had this thing about how all the rooms had to be covered in carpet. This was thirty-year-old, filthy blue pile that my roommate and I begged him to strip and replace. He refused. Our eyes itched constantly.

True story. This really happened: To suffocate the dust and mold, we spread clean, white bedsheets over the carpet. This had the effect of making the entire apartment look like a crime scene: Murder had happened, or was happening, or would happen.

Our home was murder in perpetuity.

I'd been sad lately, which was unusual. Typically, I was too pissed off to be sad. But things had been going downhill for a long time, and not just in my own life. It was like all of reality was hanging over an invisible precipice, about to tilt into something monstrous. Everyone was feeling this way. I could see it in my coworkers. I could see it on the street and in doctor's offices. We tittered with a nervous energy, like animals in tied bags about to be dropped into a river.

I was on the common room couch that night, feet propped, scrolling my screen in the dark. Pot smoke wafted from the brightly lit crack beneath my roommate Punk Rock Dean's bedroom. He and his dealer Sick Mike (whom he'd mistaken for his best friend) were getting high. I didn't like them enough to want to join in. But I did notice, in a self-conscious sort of way, that I'd been excluded. Again.

Onscreen, advertisements popped like hot corn kernels. It was impossible to distinguish one from the next. Now, they were selling some kind of flexible dildo (or maybe a face massager?). The actor said it had changed his life. He used to be worried about politics and war crimes but his face dildo had taught him how to relax. That targeted advertisement ended (Why me? Did I seem like somebody who needed a face dildo to take my mind off war crimes?). Then came a lady in big hoop earrings with black hair: *Madam Pamela.*

I'd been vaguely aware of Madam Pamela for years. She was one of many crackpots who charged exorbitant fees for psychic video readings, which she called *encounters*. These encounters had made her rich and famous. So famous that even her fans had a name: *Pam-a-maniacs.*

I don't know why I'd never recognized her before that night. She'd been a celebrity for a long time. My only explanation was that I was an oblivious person. For various reasons, and also one very specific reason, I didn't tend to look outside my life or imagine the circumstances of the people I'd once known.

But things bubble up, especially the stuff you try hardest to weigh down. What's that line?

The past isn't over. It isn't even past.

Though Pam had been pretty in high school—that kind of bland, nonthreatening, approachable pretty that the boys loved—money had made her beautiful. Her once frizzy hair was smooth, her pimply skin clear.

"Are you curious about the spirit world?" she asked, her voice soft and seductive, her body turned sideways to make her waist appear thin, her face captured from a high and flattering angle. Why do women do that? Even at forty, they can't just sell a product: they have to *sexy*-sell it. "Do you wonder what dreadful drearies whisper their stories in my ears? Have you ever been alone in a room, and suddenly felt eyes upon you? It's the creatures of the nether and soon you'll see them, too. Get your ticket to the Big Reveal on January 31st. Tell your friends, tell everyone you've ever known, my beautiful Pam-a-maniacs!" And then, somehow, she was looking just at me. Our eyes met in the dark. "Trust me," she said. "This is a revelation of biblical proportions. This is everything."

I was already mad that some jerk on my screen was telling me that she had the answers to the complex problems of a falling-apart world, a world that made less sense every day. Worse, she seemed to be trying to tell me that she could fix me personally. But what business was it of hers, that I was broken?

I despised her for that alone. But then, camera lingering, she tucked a lock of black hair behind her ear. The action reminded me of a girl from my wincing, painful past. A girl who'd hurt me so badly that I still hadn't recovered.

An asshole, in other words.

A funny thing happened right then. Every amorphous bad feeling I'd had; every sorrow, every rage... these distilled. They became a perfect arrow of blame. I swear to God, I got goosebumps.

"Fuck me. Fuck her. Madam Pamela is Pam Kowolski," I said to the dark room.

They're All Gonna Laugh at You!

Some context: Back at Sewanhaka Senior High, Pam was one of those agreeable girls everybody liked. She wore witchy black broom skirts and carried a Tarot deck to fool people into thinking she was deep. Her crew was an assortment of mid-level popular, moderately but not especially athletic norm-cores. In other words, she was Wonder Bread. Tapioca. The extra rice you get at a Chinese restaurant that you don't want.

For reasons unknown, Pam got accelerated into the AP classes senior year. Because none of her meathead friends were in these classes, and because no one who knew me liked me, we were often forced to partner up.

I was fighting a lot of demons back then. Memories of my mom were still fresh. Still, if I'm honest, I didn't mind partnering with Pam. She was a good second. She took notes in neat, very small handwriting that tended to have lots of unnecessary loops. Her numbers and letters were sometimes backward, I suspect just to piss me off. Still, she was sweet. I never felt judged.

But then one day in physics class, I made a harmless comment. She took offence and retaliated. She cut into me, mean and loud for everyone to hear. I could no longer remember exactly she'd said. But I remembered the laughter. They'd all laughed, like seeing me sliced open, my organs bleeding out, was funny.

What followed were an ugly last few months of high school. I hid in the library between classes, counting the seconds until graduation. In physics, I refused a partner and worked only by myself. People looked at me. They stared like I was a monster but I wasn't. Pam Kowolski was the monster.

The only thing that kept me going was the conviction that the dynamic between me and boring, stupid Pam Kowolski would reverse. One day, I'd become a powerful journalist, exposing corrupt corporate elites, big pharma, and government officials on the take. I'd have piles of lovers. They'd beg me to settle down and I'd say: *I'm sorry. I can't. I have a responsibility to my public.* This love loss would be the personal tragedy that propelled my career to the top. I'd be famous and rich and of more importance, I'd make a difference. Because of me, the world would be a better place.

Pretty Pam with her mousy face and nothing personality wouldn't manage nearly as well. Stumbling out from Sewanhaka High and into the big, scary world, she'd trip on her dumb-ass witch skirt. There wouldn't be any fawning teachers around to pick her back up. Her fake-nice smile wouldn't pay the bills, either. With all those backward numbers and letters, she'd make a bad assistant. In the end, she'd be lucky to get a cashier job at Western Beef. At our twentieth reunion, I'd look hot and she'd be thick-middled and pregnant with kid number five; hopefully balding, too. I'd walk up and shake her hand; glance at her name tag and act totally surprised. "You've changed so much I don't even recognize you!" I'd say.

Then I'd feel bad. I'd realize that she really was broken—brutalized by a world she'd never been strong or smart enough to navigate. I'd see that I'd inflated her value while underestimating my own: she'd never been special enough to be my enemy. I'd realize that as someone blessed with so many gifts, I should have helped her, not despised her for her limitations. What a mistake I'd made! I'd move on with grace and pity.

But life isn't always fair. I never got that opportunity to be the bigger person.

What happened that day in class with Pam left a stigma. Ever after, kids in the halls snickered. Though I never talked about it, news spread. To this day, I have no idea who told the admissions department at Northwestern University. But they found out. They rescinded their offer, claiming an anonymous employee at Sewanhaka High had alerted them to an incident in my AP physics class, in which I'd exhibited extreme psychological instability. The concerned citizen, whose name they were not at liberty to disclose, had apparently informed them that I'd never gotten over my mother's death and was at risk for self-harm. They'd followed up with the school administration and learned that the school nurse, to whom I'd been sent afterward, and additionally my guidance counselor, had filed reports.

The lady at Northwestern's admissions department said if I went through psychological counseling over the summer, the board would reconsider, but as the situation stood, they couldn't take on the liability. I'd hung up the phone, thinking: 1) Who'd ratted me out? 2) I didn't like sharing the thick markers in Art for Nonartists; I certainly wasn't about to start sharing feelings with a psychologist.

I got out of Floral Park despite all that, with a partial scholarship to SUNY New Paltz, but it was no Northwestern. They didn't care about journalism. Everybody I met was into dope, rock climbing, vinyl records, and fucking. Carabiners dangled from their sporty, rich kid backpacks and their only interest in the English language involved resurrecting dead slang words: *knocking boots, shagging, porking, railing, 5-0, smack, Roxy, Molly, Mary Jane,* etc. I mean, what the hell was wrong with these people that they couldn't just say *sex* and *drugs*?

These were not the elite crew of uber-nerds in aspirational polo shirts with plans to run for senator or write for *The New Yorker* that I'd hoped to meet in Evanston, Illinois. At New Paltz, smart was irrelevant, if also vaguely threatening. In other words, I dressed wrong, said everything wrong, and made people uncomfortable.

The one bright spot was that by going away to school, I'd freed myself from my dad and stepmom. But dorm life turned out worse. Back on Long Island, my dad had at least acknowledged my general sentience. The people at New Paltz ignored me. They took road trips without me. I had no one to sit with in the cafeteria, so I sneaked out with my tray and ate in my room. By October, my three roommates petitioned the housing office to have me removed. The dishes I'd stashed in my closet had drawn pests. I got called into the counseling office, where a lady asked me questions off a checklist and diagnosed me with an *adjustment disorder*. She then said, "Oh! You've got a note in your file about this. An *anonymous Floral Park School District employee* called us about an unfortunate incident last year. A delayed trauma response to your mother's death. Can you tell me about it?"

She'd said this like it was a eureka moment. Like, if we got to the bottom of my humiliation at the hands of Pam Kowolski, I'd be saved and loved and no longer an angry, arrogant misfit.

"Fuck you," I said. Then I dropped out.

I moved back home, where I wasn't wanted. What followed was an internship at a blogging site, supplemented by a string of menial jobs until my dad died and my stepmom kicked me out, then the steady job moving boxes at the Congo distribution center and a string of cheap apartments, the most recent of which was this place I shared with Punk Rock Dean. I was too surly to make manager, and also not very good with people. So I stayed a grunt.

Life chugged onward. I turned forty. I'd never been pretty, but now I was middle aged. If Sewanhaka High had a reunion, I wasn't invited. Without fame or even a byline, I wouldn't have gone. The world was worse. I was worse. My potential had not magically transmogrified into success, but instead continued to burn inside me, a ball of useless, scary rage over which I had less and less control. I lashed out at the poor schmucks checking out my groceries and the librarians in Elmont who insisted I use a fucking app to find books instead of just asking them. I lashed out at waiters who did everything wrong or were too slow or too casual or looked at me sideways. I lashed out at random people sitting next to me whose dumb knees were too close to mine. I lashed out at pedestrians who walked too damn slow, like: *Tra-la-la! I live in fantasy land! I have no concept right now that I'm wasting everyone's time!*

I knew it was wrong as I did it, and yet I couldn't contain it.

Recently, that rage had turned inward. I'd become slow and sad and tired. I saw myself in the mirror and wanted to shatter it. I tore up photos of myself. I burned the journals I'd been keeping since working at Congo, because twelve years later, I still hadn't written that expose on the effects of monopolistic practices on corporate, low-level employees. Because Congo wasn't my fake life. I wasn't a patrician impersonating a pleb while secretly taking excellent notes. I was a pleb. As the journals went up in smoke on the roof of my apartment and I sprayed lighter fluid into the bowl to make sure nothing survived, I understood that this, too, was crazy. The kind of behavior that characterized noir villains and movie-of-the-week murderers before they shot up trains.

I could have been someone. I could have made the world better. But a bad thing happened, first with my mom, and then with Pam. Those bad things followed me. I couldn't stand to look at them, and I couldn't jettison them, and now I was no one at all.

That winter night, in a panting, red-faced rush, the humiliation returned. And there was rich, beautiful Pam, hawking snake oil to the masses. And then the commercial was over. My streamie about parasite-fungus-zombies in the apocalypse resumed.

By then I didn't care about the parasite-fungus-zombies. As if waking up from a very deep slumber, I realized that I never had.

I rewatched the advertisement in which Pam was neither pregnant nor bald. She hadn't peaked in high school after all:

She'd been a cute bud before it fully blooms into something authentically, horribly spectacular. The woman fucking glowed.

She was me. I was her. She'd taken my life.

Without deciding to do it, I was pacing, my feet slamming the soft, white sheeted floor. I was sweating. I'd seen this in streamies —people under duress suddenly sweat so heavily it drips from their faces —but I hadn't ever before understood that it happened.

"Fuck!" I said, my eyes wet with sweat, my shirt soaked through. I thought I was just talking, not yelling, but then my landlord banged his ceiling (my floor) with what I could only assume was a broom.

Out of necessity, I calmed down. I loaded the advertisement again, zoomed in. Yes. It was true. Pam Kowolski was Madam Pamela. These were the same people.

This was real.

◉

I spent the rest of the night deep-diving Pam Kowolski in her journey from simp to global mogul. Off her website, I learned that she lived in a mansion called Split Foot, which she'd built over the ashes of the abandoned Packard Factory in Detroit, a place she claimed was the epicenter of psychic phenomena. With the help of her spirit guide, a specific invisible soul that spoke only to her, she'd opened a hole between worlds to strengthen her connection to the unknown. For instance, it could be very difficult to communicate with someone who'd been dead for fifty years. They often weren't still wandering the terrestrial plane. This hole made it easier for them to hear her when she called. Of course, lots of things heard her. This new portal wasn't purely good. She claimed that she had to be very careful about what she allowed through.

In the mornings she liked to take long swims. This was accompanied by a lame photo of a really goddamned pretty sun-dappled, Olympic-sized swimming pool. She also only ate vegan because she said *all souls matter*. The greenhouse on her property used no pesticides. You could click to find vegan recipes and gardening tips. These were accompanied, alternately, by pictures of food and pictures of Pam, looking trim and smug.

The *Philosophy* section of Pam's website delved more deeply into her psychic schtick. She said she'd always had a third eye, but that she'd honed her skill with use like a professional athlete. She said that the rules of magic and reality were undergoing a "cataclysmic shift," which she likened to the inverting of magnetic north: the reality that humanity had all come to rely upon was crumbling at an accelerated rate. Magic was gaining traction over logic.

In her videos, she was her persona, *Madam Pamela*, a woman who moaned in low tones and rolled her eyes to the back of her head when hosting *encounters*. These encounters typically involved a sad person who'd recently lost someone they loved. They'd paid Pam lots of money and agreed to be recorded. Then Pam, before introducing them to invisible, imaginary dead people, explained her cockamamie philosophy, which over the years had become a cultural phenomenon.

Dressed in hoop earrings, her voice dramatically deep, she claimed that after people died, they left invisible psychic sheddings like snake's skin. Often, they left many sheddings that reflected different times and aspects of their life journeys. These were empty, readable, and light enough to float.

Sometimes, when she searched for them using her psychic prowess, they plumped out and filled with hosts. These hosts were the spirits of the dead. Sometimes, the wrong spirits filled the casings. Sometimes, it wasn't even spirits that possessed this detritus, but something unknown. Something inhuman—that had never been human. This was why Pam's job was so risky and why she sometimes had to "break the psychic connection."

I'll give her this: She put on a good show. While watching the recordings on her site, I really did feel like something unworldly was in the room with me. The table she was sitting at tilted. Her ceiling lights flickered. She pulled clients' dead family member's names from seemingly thin air. She described their appearances, typically multiple appearances representing different "sheddings," and how they'd died. Sometimes, she shouted at the spirits, telling them they were in the wrong place, or that they were imposters. Once, she ended the reading, announcing that an evil spirit had tried to insert itself into the encounter. Her voice got deep, as if possessed by it—fighting it.

Two thirds of the time, the encounters were Hallmark Cards. By the end, the loved ones who'd hired her were reduced to weeping messes. *Thank you, Madam Pamela,* they said. *I love you, Madam Pamela,* they said. The other third, things went wrong. Something ugly got revealed, or the spirit wasn't the spirit it claimed to be, or the bereaved became hysterical.

It confused me that the show was so popular, given how often the reunions went badly. But as I combed through Reddit and Substack, I began to understand that Pam-a-Maniacs weren't showing up for the lovey-dovey stuff. They wanted the mess. The broken families. The angry ghosts.

Think about it. If somebody told you that in heaven you'd get ice cream and hugs—you'd get to finally ride that Pegasus unicorn you prayed for every night when you were six—would you believe it? Or would you get mad? Would you think they were trying to make a fool of you? But if someone told you: *It's real, but it's fucked up*, would you think: *Finally, something I can believe in*.

So they tuned into the Church of Pamela every week, thrilled by what they might find, because every episode had the excitement of a game of Russian roulette.

The hustle looked simple enough. Even if Madam Pamela's customers were randomly chosen, assistants nearby could search email handles in real time, whispering answers through a microphone in her ear. If she guessed wrong and the show went south, she could always end an encounter early due to "demonic insertion."

Lately, Pam had added a new attraction to her empire. She claimed to have discovered the means by which to share her abilities. She planned to reveal that secret on a special pay-per-view livestream. People who tuned in would see ghost casings, spirits, long-gone loved ones, demons—everything that she saw.

This announcement incited a global frenzy. Fans went bananas. All people could talk about was: *Is it real? If you could see the dead, would you want to? Is it fake? Is she crazy? Sign me up!* Advance ticket sales were at 200 million units, and over a billion dollars. The thing about suckers; they're born every minute.

Hate can be invigorating. I had fun researching Pam. I hadn't used my brain in years. Hadn't written seriously in north of a decade. It felt impossibly serendipitous. A perfect story had landed right in my lap. I thought right away of my old boss Tom Einhorn at Fuckfeed.com, the last online magazine that supported long form articles written by human journalists. When I left the company, we'd both been unpublished interns. Over the years of layoffs and contractions, he'd gotten promoted and was now editor in chief.

As soon as dawn arrived, I uploaded a fake doctor's note to Congo, saying I had influenza strain B and couldn't come to work. Then I called Tom.

"Jan?" he asked, his voice groggy. I'd never liked to be called Jan. He'd never asked. Sometimes it was *Jan-O*, or *Jan-a-lana-ding-dong*. Really. He really did this.

"I've got a story. I'm sending the pitch right now," I told him. "Madam Pamela."

"Madam Pamela? She's dope! I inhale that show every week like it's a single malt. Scripted streamies are done-zo. Me and my peeps're all about the real dirt. The fa-shizzle! Secrets and skeletons in closets. Are you so stoked for the Big Reveal?" Tom asked. "We got our tickets, Jan-o! I don't care if it's on the level or it's grocery store sea moneys. This is the cultural event of the century!"

Like all trustafarians, Tom lived in Brooklyn and wore very tight suits and too white sneakers. He bleached his gray hair, then gelled it so it stood straight up. His wife was ten years younger and hot. Her boobs were giant because she was still nursing their five-year-old twins, who were too goddamned old to be nursed. I knew this, not because I'd ever been to his house, but because he posted constantly on social media.

"You'll notice her website doesn't offer refunds," I said.

"What?" Tom asked. "Who'd want a refund? We're gonna be talking about this reveal for a hundred years."

"Her real name's Pam Kowolski. We went to high school together. She seems all nice, Tom, but I know her. She's a con. It's all a con."

"Can you get an interview?" he asked.

Famously, Madam Pamela didn't give interviews. "Sure," I lied. "She and I go way back."

"For real?" he asked, then lowered his voice. "Fuckfeed's not hot lately. Clicks are down. People aren't... they're not acting how they used to. We can't predict their behaviors using any of our algorithms. Have you noticed that? The way people aren't acting like you'd expect?"

I shook my head into the phone. I never noticed or liked people enough to establish their patterns.

"Anyway, this could really help our revenue stream. You're sure you can get an interview?"

"Definitely," I promised.

"Okay. This could jam, baby! Just don't get too smart. Like, if you're tempted to use the word zeitgeist, walk away from your computer. No one wants that egghead stuff. That's why you didn't work out around here. Slam her, suck up to her, I don't care. Just get the click-bait. I can't pay upfront. Any expense for you is out of pocket. But I can give you a percent based on engagement. I'm looking at your pitch now and I'll reply with the contract."

"Great!" I said.

"You're the best, Jan-o!" he said.

"No you are, Tom! You're the best!" I answered, because Tom had zero ear for sarcasm.

First Contact

Later that morning, Punk Rock Dean and Sick Mike staggered out from Dean's bedroom. Dean had a shift at Congo and Sick Mike had drugs to deliver or his own house to crash in, or a homeless person to punch, or whatever the hell it was he did on his own dime.

Sick Mike gave me the stink eye as he gathered his backpack and winter parka, both of which were made of reflective material, like he was afraid of getting hit by a car at night, or else they were twenty-year-old gifts from his mom.

"Janet," he said, in a way that sounded like both an acknowledgment and an accusation.

You ever get that feeling people have been talking about you, and not saying very nice things? I looked at them both for a long beat. "Mike," I said.

Then he was gone.

That left my actual roommate, Punk Rock Dean. Up until his late 50s, he'd been lead guitar and vocals for a moderately successful Clash cover band. But life (marriages, addiction, money troubles, kids) got in the way. The band broke up. Poverty forced him into a day job at Congo. He posted an ad for a roommate on the employee lounge bulletin board. I'd been living in a basement apartment at the time, sharing a hall bathroom with four other people.

I jumped.

Dean was fastidious in his taste and in his appearance. He gelled his gray hair Einstein wild, painted his fingernails black, wore black band t-shirts (mostly Nirvana), and professed not to *give a shite*, often in a fake British accent. For these reasons, I called him Punk Rock Dean. This bothered him greatly because, like most aging punk rockers who should have made better long term financial plans, he gave a shite about everything, particularly the stupid stuff, like whose cereal belonged to whom and whether the kitchen counter had been adequately wiped of crumbs. Nearly every morning, I discovered the tennis shoes I'd taken off in front of the big screen the night before deposited before my closed door, along with whatever stray pen or other personal item I'd dared abandon instead of properly stashing.

I'm erasing you from the crime scene!

Neither of us said hello that morning. Dean took his very many vitamins while simultaneously wet-coughing. He blamed his chronic cough on the carpet, though I suspected it was also the constant smoking. Meanwhile, I reposed on the couch like a dare: would it concern him that I was skipping out on work, which might make me short on rent?

Like all relationships, the two of us had started out optimistic. I'm not sure what went wrong. I can only say that nothing went right. There was never a moment when we laughed uproariously. Dean never spotted me an extra token for the laundry. I never gave him any of the trinkets from the remainder bin at work. He liked the movie *Spinal Tap*, which he watched nearly every night. He believed in palmistry and tarot, often reading his own cards by candlelight. Oddly, he also loved period romance, particularly Jane Austin. I found these obsessions stupid.

Sometimes, he had old man smell. You know that smell.

Relations can't stay in limbo forever. Eventually, a jury decides using the information it's been given. In absence of ever getting along, we came to the joint conclusion that Dean did not like me, and I did not like him. The silence in our home, once expectant, turned hostile.

Over the last month or so, the tension between us had gotten really bad. I had the feeling he'd erase me if he could. Obliterate me. Stuff my body and everything I owned under a white sheet with all the other garbage.

To my great relief, he left with haste.

◉

I spent the day combing through Pam's online presence, including legal proceedings attached to her name. It was pretty much what you'd expect. Her ex-husband and her dad both sued for cuts of her company and lost. A few encounter subjects with bad outcomes sued, too. These were settled out of court.

Comments in several anonymous chatroom threads expressed concern that the world wasn't ready for her Big Reveal. It might break reality. These chains included photos of posters' doomsday prepped basements and stories about times they'd encountered real ghosts.

An entire thread with more than a thousand comments examined the uptick in suicide over the last several years and tried to link it to Madam Pamela's Split Foot portal. The original poster believed that when she opened it, she'd let through something malignant. The most sensitive people in the population, like canaries in coal mines, hadn't needed to see these spirits, like Pam could do. They'd *felt* them. And this had driven them to self-murder.

Commenters posted about family members and friends they'd lost to the suicide blight. The stories were upsetting and reminded me too much of my mom, so I stopped reading them and investigated from a numbers perspective. According to the US census, suicide was at an all-time high. Since the announcement of her Big Reveal, the numbers had grown exponentially. Suicide now beat cancer and heart disease as a leading cause of death. In some confined pockets of society, like apartment complexes and small towns, suicide rates were as high as 10% of the adult population. One hopeless act gave people ideas and led to more suicides until it was a political statement, a fad, a blight, a social disease.

As I read, the sun got higher, midday rays pushing through the common room. I sent an email to Pam's website:

> *Hi! You probably don't remember me, but we went to school together. Congratulations on all your success! It's amazing! I'm surprised and stunned. Anywho! I'm writing an article about the Madam Pamela phenomenon for Fuckedfeed.com and I was wondering if you might be interested in an interview? I'd love to help you with some pre-publicity with your big reveal. What is it, anyway? Can you tell me?*

Sincerely,
Janet Chow

A minute later, two new messages appeared in my in-box. The first was a reply from Pam's assistant:

Thank you for your interest in Madam Pamela. Attached is a press kit.

This was the answer I'd anticipated. It nonetheless drove me totally fucking insane. What kind of ridiculous fucking world was I living in, that someone like Pam Kowalski could blow me off like I was nobody?

The second email was from Tom:

Jannie—
Cool reconnecting! I remember worrying about you when you left but you're like a cat, always landing on your feet!!! I was talking to my wife. She's a huge Pam-a-Maniac fan. An OBSESSED true believer. But she's INSANELY worried about the Big Reveal. She thinks Pam's lost touch, that it might hurt people (see attached). But she also can't wait to watch. Makes me think this article could be FIRE. Tsss! Hot, hot, hot!

The attached is confidential. My wife's friend is the head of Madam Pamela's fan club (Captain Pam-A-Maniac!) and saved this encounter even though it was scrubbed from the internet. The Madam Pamela industrial complex is rigorous and specific about its content. There may be more videos like these. No way to tell. Trigger warning, here.

Don't watch this if you can't handle gory.
Be well,
Tom

I read this and had two reactions: 1) Gory??? 2) Was *be well* the new wolf whistle of the modern age? It essentially assumed the opposite: Nothing's well, so remember your nuclear fallout umbrella and hurricane boots. Hope you don't die of plague before our next communication. Also, I take zero responsibility for you, another human being on this earth. It's every asshat for himself.

Before viewing the encounter, I got up for a snack. I toasted a slice of Dean's bread and chased it with one of his anti-cancer COQ vitamins, which had a tasty sugary coating.

Then I watched. Below is my annotated transcription.

Madam Pamela's "Encounter" with Sunny Jackson, March 15, 2020, 9pm EST:

A younger, moonier-faced Madam Pamela who more closely resembles Pam Kowolski from high school sits on a red velvet chair. In front of her is a low table with candles lit bright. This is when she's still in a one-bedroom flat on Long Island: before her career takes off—she doesn't have her act down. She's sporting a frilly dress dotted with cartoon red hearts instead of her trademark black silk. It's hard to take her seriously.

Madam Pamela: Greetings, fellow travelers of the occult. By now you know the drill. If you like what you see, click right and send cash. If you don't, you know where you can go. Danny—do we have any contenders?

Danny: (OS) Seven entrants, Pammie.

This is early in her career. By 2025, her shows typically have tens of thousands of entrants and nobody calls her Pammie.

Madam Pamela: They're onscreen—everyone can see them?

Danny (OS, sounding slightly bored): Affirmative.

Madam Pamela (nervous, thrown by this poor showing): Great. Let the viewers—there's thirty-two of you? Wow, I'm really losing traction. Let the viewers decide. Vote left. There's a poll.

It's an amateur operation. You get the feeling this is a small kitchen table over which she's thrown a caftan knit by her Great Aunt Hildie. As she waits, she picks something green from between her teeth and swallows it.

Danny: Okay—it's number four—Sunny Jackson from Oceanside, California. Have you ever met Sunny before right now, Pammie?

Madam: No. I have not.

Sunny Jackson (wildly excited): Oh, my God. OMG.

The screen splits and a heavyset blonde with bald patches along her temples appears. She's got wide, intense eyes. But there's something vacant about them.

Sunny: Jesus, Mary, and Joseph. Mary Magdalene, Luke, Mark John, and Matthew. Matthew the Baptist. I mean John the Baptist! They're all paying witness to your power. The saints of yesterday bow before you! The saints of tomorrow lean back to know you! This is the moment. You are the change. The end and the beginning and the ever shall believeth in you—

Madam Pamela puts Sunny on mute, raises an eyebrow at the camera. It's funny. I want to say it's mean because she's Pam and she sucks, but it's not mean. It's playful. Viewers rain down smiley faces.

Madam: Oh, boy, Sunny Jackson from Oceanside, California. That's so many saints! I'm not sure I've earned all that just yet but thank you. Now, you're here because you want to connect with someone who has passed. Is that right?

Sunny hasn't stopped talking even though she's been muted. Her lips continue to move. Her expression remains sweet, but there's still that vacancy. Like parts of her person have been scraped away and the rest of her is maniacally covering for that absence, pretending everything's abso-fucking-lutely fantastic!

I watch this piece of film over and over, and every time I read her lips, I get the same thing. It looks like she's saying—

Sunny Jackson: —Blood and shit. I'll kill you all. Be—

Then she's unmuted, and it's like some kind of trick of sound or light or reality, because she continues without stopping, only now it's fawning and innocuous—

Sunny Jackson: —lieve we're here! I can't believe this is really happening. I've been watching you from day one.

Sunny's such a simpleton that it seems impossible. And yet... What words rhyme with blood, shit, *and* kill?

Madam: That's me! Madam Pamela. Now, Sunny, who are we seeking today?

Sunny: We're talking right now. Through the internet. I'm talking to Madam Pamela. I'm a Pam-a-maniac!

Madam: Yup. Three deep breaths, then tell me the reason you reached out.

Sunny complies, breathing slow and deep. When she's done, she's calmer but her eyes are wet with dumb intensity, like a surprised deer.

Sunny: I'm here because of my daughter and I need you to witness what I'm about to do. It's the only way I'll know it's real—

Sunny reaches to the side as if to show us something off camera—

Madam: Stop! No pictures, please. What about your daughter?

Sunny: I need you to see her. Could you find her for me?

Madam: That's my job, Sunny.

Sunny: Now? You're going to find her right now?

Madam smiles kindly at Sunny and closes her eyes. The candles go out. In freeze frame, I can see the edges of a fan to her right, which Danny's waving.

Madam: I see her. She was little, maybe three. Hit by a car?

Sunny (thrilled; hysterical): Yes. OMG.

There's something very off about Sunny. I get the feeling that she's faking her reaction and isn't surprised at all. But she also doesn't seem present or engaged enough for this to be any kind of plot. It's just odd.

Madam: The line connecting the two of you isn't the same color. Did something happen to come between you?

Sunny: I don't think so.

Madam Pamela sneers. She's explained this trademark expression (that has become an omnipresent meme) as accidental resting bitch face.

Madam: Don't pretend. I can tell something happened.

This isn't typical of Madam Pamela's later encounters—the ones she keeps in syndication. She's usually understanding: never calls anyone out. At her confrontational words, Sunny starts crying. She doesn't make any noise. Tears just fall. Their faces are side-by-side onscreen. Behind Sunny, I note chipped blue paint. She's sitting on a floor, balancing her screen on her lap. It feels like this might be a public place. A bus station or homeless shelter.

Sunny: Yes. She was taken away sometimes. She lived with some people called Colbridges and some other people, too.

Madam: She was hit by a car?

Sunny: Yes.

Madam: Have I ever met you before? Have you told me anything about yourself?

Sunny: No.

Madam: I have your daughter here. Her name is Crystal?

Sunny: Yes.

Madam: She's...

Madam Pamela's thick brows roll together. The sweetheart dress she's wearing suddenly seems anachronistic, and it occurs to me that someone gave her bad advice. They told her to ditch the broom skirts and smile more. But it's wrong, somehow. Pam was a respectable, fake-serious, phony, not a, heart-wearing, giggling phony.

Sunny's screen tilts momentarily and now I'm sure it's a bus station. I can just see the lit-up bathroom sign at the top right of the screen—the geometric shape of a woman in a dress with the words: ticketed passengers only *right below.*

Sunny: What? She's what?

Madam: Why did you contact me today?

Sunny: I miss her.

Madam: Is that true?

Sunny: Yes.

Madam: She's been haunting you, hasn't she? Moving things, visiting your waking dreams.

Sunny: I miss her. Does she know? I think she doesn't know or she wouldn't act like this.

Madam: You shouldn't have contacted me.

Madam Pamela's lips draw into a rictus grin.

Sunny: Please. What's she saying?

Madam: I started doing this to this to help people. I have a gift and I'll go crazy if I don't use it. I tried working for the police. It was too upsetting. It made me sick. So, I started doing this because these reunions can be healing. But this won't heal you. Why do you want this?

Madam Pamela pauses, allowing Sunny room to respond. She doesn't. There's a wariness, a knowing between the two of them that they haven't yet shared with the rest of us.

Madam: She's angry, Sunny. But you know that because she's been haunting you.

Sunny doesn't appear as distressed as she ought to—as a person hearing that their dead kid hates them on live stream. She's disturbingly, almost gallingly sanguine.

Sunny: You're wrong. I was the best mom.

Madam: You honestly want to talk to her right now. You understand that once I invite them in, I don't always have control?

Sunny: I want to know she can see me. I want her to witness. I want you all to witness. Please let me talk to her.

Madam Pamela closes her eyes and hums. It's theatrics. Light-as-a-feather kid stuff. The lights dim.

Her countenance changes. Her eyes and lips scrunch and she hunches. She captures the way a toddler rocks in their chair, the way they play with their fingers as if still getting used to having them. Even for a skeptic like me, this change feels uncanny.

Madam *(in babytalk):* You pushed me, Mommy.

Here's the crazy part. The lights on Sunny's end at the bus station flicker, like an infection is spreading from one screen to the other.

Sunny: Baby? Do you see me? Look at me!

Still vacant, Sunny lifts something offscreen. We see that it wasn't a photo. There's a loud BANG!

A kind of cognitive dissonance happens. It takes a moment before I place the sound as gunshot, before I understand that the fast-reeling thing quickly vanishing from the inset screen is Sunny's blown-off head.

"Holy shit," I say in my apartment, where the sun has set, and strangely, coincidentally, the lights flicker. What's worse, the video's still running. One half of the screen is bloodsplattered blue wall and ambient screams. The other half is Madam Pamela. Slowly, still in character as that murdered toddler, the edges of Pam's mouth twist into a grin.

End of video.

◉

Dean stomped around that night. He was loud on the phone with Sick Mike, whom he really needed to realize was not his friend, but a guy who overcharged him for high THC weed that he could have gotten much cheaper at Congo using his employee discount.

"Yeah, it's shite," Punk Rock Dean said, coughing wet and rustling through the kitchen like a confused bear trying to work jar lids for the first time. "Some bootlicker nabbed it instead.... No. It's my age. It's ageism."

So, he'd lost the promotion. He'd been plotting to get it in secret for a while now, but I'd known about it because he was bad at keeping secrets. The job included a pay raise with enough money to kick me out on my ass. For obvious reasons, I was relieved.

Preoccupied by the video I'd just watched, I stayed on the couch as he squawked his frustration, ultimately agreeing to buy twice his regular amount from Sick Mike, who'd be over soon.

...Had simpleton Pam Kowolski from high school pretended to be possessed by a deranged, murdered toddler? Had she driven that white trash mom to suicide? What the hell kind of person was I dealing with?

There were more squawks. Mike appeared, like he'd beamed himself to our front door. They got high in the kitchen, side-eyeing me but not actually speaking to me. I wasn't wanted and I knew it, but I was afraid to be alone after watching a woman murder herself on my screen, so I stayed on the couch. Dean passed Mike a stack of wrinkled bills and a jar of coins, which he shoved into his backpack like Smeagol stealing the ring of doom. Having gotten what he wanted, he left.

People say pot mellows them. That's probably true. But if you've been using for years—decades, even—it does the opposite. It carves something out of you over time, and you know it. You know you're missing that thing. You know you're less than you used to be. And you're mad about it.

Though Dean and I didn't get along, until now this disharmony had mostly expressed itself as avoidance. Nobody wants their home to be a place of tumult. But that night, Dean turned his furious, red-veined eyes to me, and I could see that our peace was about to end.

"Thief," he said.

Turned out, he'd set a trap, leaving stray hairs in his private cupboard. These had been disturbed. I'd eaten his toast and vitamins! I was a sneak! An enemy in his sanctuary! How could I be such a monster?

I considered explaining that yeah, I was a thief. But only of small things. It's unmooring to live in a home where you're not supposed to touch or *be* or leave traces of yourself. If you don't move condiments when no one's looking, or leave your underpants in front of the toilet, or steal small objects, maybe you don't exist.

"You're shite!" he said in that bad, made-up Cockney. "No one likes you."

Most people aren't good with confrontation. It catches them on their back feet and they tend to bite back. They're not their best selves. I'd noticed this. Though I liked to think of myself as exceptional, in this case I was like most people. "Yeah," I said. "Sucks for you, 'cause I got squatters rights…. The bootlicker didn't get the job because he's young. He got it because he's not high all the time. Keep it up and you'll give yourself lung cancer. With that cough, you probably have cancer already."

Tears of rage appeared at the corners of Dean's eyes. He smeared his too pale face with both hands, as if to erase it, or himself, or the moment, or me, or maybe even this terrible situation, in which two adults were fighting literally over scraps.

Pretty soon, he was back in his room getting high. I heard his streamie, tuned to tonight's live Madam Pamela encounter.

I had the notion I might knock and apologize, or at least discuss the problem further (did Dean have any idea how weird it was to boobytrap bread? And seriously, the cough and the vaping were connected. He had to know that, right? Had he considered spending his money on a doctor and not Sick Mike?). But I had no idea how to broach such things with a red-eyed rage monster with a fake cockney accent that might have been cute when he was thirty, but at sixty made him seem unhinged.

That night, sounds felt too loud, creaks in the floors malignant. Everything was off and wrong, like Sunny Jackson's empty eyes, like Madam Pamela grinning a child's conscienceless grin, like Dean after too many hits. I thought of my mom at a kitchen table, counting pills on the last day of her life. I thought of Pam, turning on me. All of these conflated, frightening and monstrous.

I tore through the closed things in my room—closets and drawers—feeling like a presence was there with me. I pushed around the plastic crates under my bed. I flipped my hamper full of Congo-regulation tan khakis and green collar shirts.

Nothing. But something. I felt something behind me, looking over my shoulder, breathing on the back of my neck…

Too jacked to sleep, I watched the Sunny Jackson video again. At minute nine, sixteen seconds, I froze the frame. In it, Pam's eyes shift. It's that moment right before her countenance changes into that of a little kid. She appears to be seeing something just off camera. Suddenly, though the video's paused, something flits.

The lights in my bedroom blinked. For a moment, it felt as if the thing had followed me through the screen. And in my mind, laughter. A classroom full of all the people I'd ever known, mocking me.

She Must Have it Wrong

The next morning, I tried to get out of the house before Dean, but he'd evidently had the same idea. So we left together. I ducked into a store and bought gum to let him get ahead, but we wound up on the same company bus, standing-room only. I was smooshed next to Punk Rock Dean, except no one at Congo knew he was Punk Rock because we all wore the same uniform and that safety pin had infected his earlobe and he'd had to take it out.

The Congo center was a high-ceilinged hangar that took up about three city blocks. Once the bus stopped, we went our separate ways. As soon as I punched in, I put on my headset, which informed me which item to pull and from where via an algorithm. A man's AI voice instructed me to turn left or right or walk three paces and look up to bin four. This went on all day. I tuned the background music to classical and tried to go with the flow. You ever see animals stuck in cages during the day? Rabbits or hamsters or guinea pigs or even dogs? They turn off. It's like they forget they're alive.

For twelve years, I'd been doing this at work; forgetting I was alive.

But today, time inched sleepily, second-by-second. I was thinking of Pam. In the early part of that video, I'd worried that I'd judged her harshly. She'd been funny. I'd forgotten that she was funny. Also, who was I to judge a woman for making a living? But then she'd grinned. Even after Sunny Jackson blew off her own head, she'd kept grinning. In the face of something so grotesque, what kind of person keeps up an act like that?

So, what next? I had a story due, and due soon.

I needed an interview. I'd have to write Pam a second note when I got home. Something that would provoke a reaction. Additionally, I could track down Sunny Jackson's family as well as former Madam Pamela employees like her ex-husband, Danny, who'd been her first cameraperson. I could contact the people who'd sued her. For background, I'd need to get in touch with Pam's old teachers, friends, and family. This part made me nervous. Sweaty nervous. These people hadn't just known Pam twenty years ago; they'd known me.

Because I'd called in sick the day before, I stayed for a double shift to make up the lost hours and also to avoid Dean. By the end of my second shift, sixteen hours had passed and my back was throbbing. "Please remember your happiness App employee discount entitles you to three free sessions per month," the AI told me as I punched out. And then, strangely, its voice changed, lilting upward. "Bye, Janet. Take good care," it said, and it sounded just like my mom, back when I'd been little, leaving the house for school.

I stopped, confused. An upgrade? Morale in distribution centers was low lately. Management was always testing new interfaces, searching for the ones that maximized efficiency. Were they playing with the algorithm to make us more productive? Had I imagined that the voice sounded just like my mom?

That voice was still fresh on my mind when I got home, which maybe explained the hotheaded letter I sent off to Pam Kowolski via her assistant:

Dear Pamela,

I saw what you did to Sunny Jackson. You're a murderer. Your powers are bullshit. The big reveal is bullshit. I'm going to prove it before you have the chance to hurt more innocent people. Fuckfeed.com has given me its every resource to destroy you. You might have fooled everyone else, but I see you. I'm watching you and soon the whole world will know.

Sincerely,
Janet Chow (I sat next to you in like, ten classes and you were the shittiest speller in the whole school)

Ten seconds after I sent it, I thought: *That was excessive.*

The rest of the week was rough. Still without speaking to me, Punk Rock Dean declared an all-out war. He padlocked the cabinets. Lacking the necessary skills to address the situation, I ignored it.

At night and during lunch breaks, I worked on my story. It turned out that Sunny Jackson didn't have surviving relatives. I tried to find her deceased daughter's foster family but they weren't listed, either. I did get in touch with Pam's ex-husband, Danny Rizzoli. *I have so many things to tell you about that crazy bitch*, Danny wrote, a line that gave me literal goosebumps when it appeared on my screen. He wanted money wired directly into his account before he'd agree to go on record. I asked Tom Einhorn at Fuckfeed for a spending account. He declined. So I looked around my room for something to hock. But I didn't own anything valuable.

Of our former teachers who were still living (disturbingly, about half were dead from old age, accidents, cancer, and suicide), most said they didn't remember Pam and were surprised to learn that she and Madam Pamela were the same person. From social media, I found Pam's former white bread, norm-core friend crew. They still lived on Long Island. Their kids went to school together, they celebrated birthdays together. I knew this because all they did was post online pictures about their perfect, stupid-ass lives. Only one of them got back to me. Either because they remembered me and still hated me, or because Pam was in contact with them and had forwarded my shamefully mean email *(I see you. I'm watching you.)*, that person wrote: who's Pam Kowolski?

You know what's worse than being ignored or secretly mocked? Getting gaslit. I mean, what the hell?

My shift days passed. I ate at separate times from Dean, who smoked more pot and coughed more than usual. On the streamies, Madam Pamela's publicity machine entered high gear. All over the city, billboards advertised her Big Reveal. Stickers of her face with QR order codes were slapped across every wall and store in my neighborhood. Tiny screens were tuned to syndicated episodes of her shows. Wherever I went, I heard her voice.

I received replies from two of the former teachers I'd contacted. Both agreed to go on record. One of them was the AP physics teacher in whose class my humiliation had occurred. I'd been afraid to write to her in the first place. Terrified, in fact. You know when you stand over a steep ledge and your stomach flops? I had that feeling, even down to my fingertips as I'd typed. Her response was this:

January 12, 2031,

Dear Janet,

What a pleasure to hear from you! You were one of my most promising students. I'd love to meet up and talk any time, about any subject under the sun.

Sincerely,
Ms. Anita Blake

Ms. Blake. Not Anita. Even twenty years later, she'd kept the formality. Though most aspects of my past were hazy, I tried to remember something about her: the appearance of her classroom, or some old assignment, or even the color of her skin. I could not. It was all a blank. A hole.

It occurred to me that this was disturbing. Did other people have such gaps in their memories? Probably not. It occurred to me that this wasn't just disturbing; it was scary.

I didn't reply for another twenty-four hours. I was afraid that if I met with Blake, I'd learn something terrible about myself. Or worse, she'd be mean. But then I gave myself a pep talk. A bad thing had happened to me, first with my mom, and then in Blake's class. But that was the past. It was dead and couldn't hurt me. If I wanted a byline, this article was my last chance.

I found Ms. Blake in a back booth at the Carle Place Diner on Old Country Road. She sat straight, with impossibly good posture, and seemed more alive than everyone else in the joint, who was bent over a device, skin dull and jaundiced. I'd gotten used to people looking this way—sickly. Ruddy Ms. Blake was a stark contrast.

My heart pounded as I approached. I could almost hear the laughter from that day more than twenty years ago. She'd been there, hadn't she? She'd witnessed it? I couldn't remember. Didn't *want* to remember.

Blake wore a yellow pantsuit and fake pearls. She didn't look much older than when she'd been my teacher, though by now she had to be in her late seventies. We caught up in a stilted, awkward way while muzak versions of old songs played.

She remembered Pam. "Good student," she said. "Sad case, though. No mom and her dad wasn't much in the picture, though I think she lived with him…. Her clothes always carried the whiff of something stale. Not enough to be off-putting. More, the way you'd imagine an absent-minded genius to smell."

I passed over a screenshot of Pam's high school yearbook photo. "Are you sure we're talking about the same person? Pam always looked great and had a boyfriend," I said. "And I don't remember her ever smelling like mothballs or a mousey house."

Ms. Blake examined the photo with two hands like it was important. Ran her fingers down along Pam's left cheek. I should not have been bothered by this, made jealous by it. "Yes, that's her. She was sad. Very bright and very sad."

"She didn't have a mom?" I felt as if Ms. Blake had confused the two of us. I thought of my mom, then, counting pills at a table amidst television soundtrack laughter. "I was the one without a mom. I had to do my own laundry."

Ms. Blake squinted, like she was looking extra close for something inside me but couldn't find it. I felt the absence somehow, as if I'd failed her. "You had that in common. In her case, I think it was abandonment."

I pictured Pam how I remembered her, smiling and waving at people in Sewanhaka's halls. She'd never seemed like the kind of person who'd been carrying tragedy. But perhaps she hadn't been carrying it. Perhaps the reason she'd seemed happy was because she'd truly been happy; a flimsy, insubstantial person, she'd lacked the depth to grieve her mother's absence.

"What kind of story are you writing?" she asked as she handed back my phone.

I remembered, then, that Ms. Blake had taught us about the discovery of relativity. How it had once been dangerous, as revolutionary as learning that the earth wasn't the center of the solar system. How lots of these super smart guys had killed themselves after spending years trying to disprove the implications of particle/wave duality and the elasticity of space-time. They'd thought one thing, and it had literally killed them to imagine they were so wrong about the world. These lessons had annoyed me. I'd wanted to cover the test material, get my five on the AP exam and move on. Blake could impart messages of pop psychology and social justice when she named her class: Useless facts that will not be on the exam.

I figured Blake would react badly to learning that I was writing a hatchet piece. "I'm still finding my story. I'm open to what develops, so any detail you tell me is useful. What can you tell me about these abilities Pam claims to have? Did anything uncanny ever occur when she was nearby?"

She ate her grilled, three-cheese sandwich neatly, one hand in her lap, and didn't answer until she was done. "What do *you* think about Madam Pamela?"

"I'm impartial," I said.

"Have you seen her since high school?"

I blushed, shook my head. No, I hadn't seen her.

"You must have an interest. Why else would you write the article?"

I had the idea she wasn't going to tell me anything more unless I showed some of my cards. Around us, a slow, lyric-less Nine Inch Nails' "Animal" played. "I feel like it's irresponsible, selling psychic encounters. It hurts people. It hurts the world," I said.

"How is it bad for the world?" she asked, and I could sense she wasn't trying to argue with me. Like all good teachers, she probably wanted to help me articulate my thesis.

"She's trying to say that because the world is falling apart, that reality is falling apart, but that's not true. Reality's reality. More people are believing in magic because more people are vulnerable. But believing in the wrong thing leads to missed opportunities. Like my roommate. I have a roommate. I'm not married." I said this like a confession. Like if she judged me for it, I'd start crying. It stunned me, that my voice had suddenly gone so raw. I was unaccustomed to human interaction.

"Me, too!" She said. "I hate living alone."

"Oh. Your husband?"

"Wife. She died. So now I have a roommate. My nephew. I like hearing noise around the apartment."

I nodded, surprised her answers hadn't been *husband* or *house*. "Oh," I said. "My roommate takes vitamins and sees healers for his cough. He watches Madam Pamela. Meanwhile… I think he might have cancer," I said. Having articulated this thought for the first time, and hearing it, I realized I believed it. Punk Rock Dean might have cancer. "People think praying will save them," I continued. "But that's not how it works. We have to save ourselves."

"Yes," she agreed. "I like this reasoning, Janet."

"I don't think all this is happening because people are stupid. Well, they're a little stupid. But mostly it's because they're tired. I'm tired," I said.

"You are?" she asked.

Seconds passed in silence. I couldn't remember the last time someone had asked me a real question and waited for my answer. Unexpected tears filled my eyes. I thought about my mom. Not my real mom, who'd always frightened me, but the mom I wished I'd had. A mom like this woman I was having lunch with.

"Yeah. It's hard to keep going. It's hard to keep trying when you feel like you're being held down. For a long time, I stopped trying. But then I saw Pam Kowolski on my stream one night and I just had to write this article."

"That's wonderful. I'm glad," she said. "But what's been holding you down?" she asked. Around us wasn't much chatter. People were mostly looking at screens. I felt very raw. I was afraid, somehow, that she'd see through me. She'd know that I wasn't nice, that I wasn't writing this article to change the world or stop magical thinking. I just wanted to hurt Pam.

I thought of my mom's pills on the kitchen table, and a laugh track, because sometimes buried things float. "You name it. Everything I've come from, everybody I've known. High school. College. The world. The system. …Other people hold me down," I said.

"Do they? But this decision to write about magical thinking using Pam as an example is wonderful," she said, and I felt like I was back in school again, young and full of promise. Eager to prove and impress. "She's an excellent subject. Very complex."

"I watched a video where a woman committed suicide because of her," I said. "These bereaved customers want reassurance. But she lies. She gets them addicted to the notion of magic—her product—instead of helping them move on."

Ms. Blake nodded thoughtfully. "Agreed."

"People don't see it," I said. "But what will happen with her Big Reveal? People are literally killing themselves, they're so upset. They need to know she's lying. She has to be exposed before more people get hurt."

"I love this and I love that you're so engaged in the work," she said. "But I have one question: what if Pamela Kowolski's abilities are real?"

"They're not," I said.

Ms. Blake smiled thin and tight. Except inside the dry cracks of her skin, her pink lipstick had mostly smeared away. It made her look old. "But just suppose everything she claims is true. Would she still be wrong to tell us about it? Was Oppenheimer wrong to share his atomic bomb?"

"Get outta here," I said.

Ms. Blake's smile stayed tight. "Janet, do you remember my lessons about particle-wave duality?"

I nodded. I remembered very well. It occurred to me that this meant she'd been a good teacher.

"You said before that reality is reality. But what if it's not? What if the rules really are changing? All over the world, people are claiming this is happening. Scientists in Moscow, real scientists, are claiming that the speed of light is no longer 86,000 meters per second squared. They say falling objects no longer accelerate at a constant. In India, they're saying they see the dead."

"They're hysterical," I said. "Pam made them sick and the tech industrial complex exacerbated that sickness for click bait ad revenue."

"Good argument," she said, and I had the strangest feeling she disagreed with me.

"Hey! You never answered my question!"

She gave me a teacherly, quizzical look. The kind where they know the answer but are making you ask the question, anyway. I liked her—she'd shown up on her own dime and her own time to help me out—but this game was wearing thin.

"My question: Did you ever witness the supernatural in her presence back in high school?"

Blake's smile faltered. She lowered her voice and bent down a little, like she was sharing a secret. "You really don't remember? I have to be honest, I thought that was some of the reason you wanted to meet."

A sweaty, nervous warmth rose up from my stomach and spread across my face. "I don't know what you're talking about."

Squinting, once again seeming to look for something inside me, she caught my eyes. "I must have it wrong. I thought it was you. But maybe it was someone else."

"What do you have wrong?" I felt myself panting. Heard it in the catching of my voice. I had the notion that the thing that had come through my screen when I'd been watching the Sunny Jackson video had followed me to this restaurant. It was watching. It knew all the things I didn't remember because it had always been watching. Only now, it was close. It was strong.

…Had Ms. Blake laughed at me, too, back on that day?

"Tell me," I said, but she hesitated, like she thought I was too fragile to hear whatever she was about to say. A knowingness passed between us, and I could tell she was thinking about what happened—the way Pam had humiliated me.

So she'd been there, after all.

Not very subtly, she pivoted. "I'll have to check my old journals and get back to you. But in the meantime, Janet, congratulations on becoming a writer! I always knew you'd do something great."

I can't explain the anger I felt, only that it reared, intense and hot.

"But what happened? What's this uncanny thing about Pam Kowolski that you think I'm crazy not to remember?"

Ms. Blake took a bite of her sandwich. Made a point of chewing for too long. It occurred to me for the first time, because I'd never allowed myself to think about it before, that as the only possible adult who could have witnessed my humiliation that day, she was the anonymous reporter.

"Tell me!"

"I'll read my journals and get back to you." Her tone went flat and without warmth.

The music was a kind of soporific. The people all around us looked dead. I felt, suddenly, like the world was wrong. Like everything bad was swelling up from deep below. "I don't think you understand—this is my shot. My career. You hurt me once. It had to be you. Now's your chance to make up for it. I'm asking you for help."

"Hurt you?"

"You know what you did," I said, because I couldn't say it. Couldn't voice the humiliation to which my blackballing was connected. It had to be her. Who else could it have been?

Ms. Blake's frozen smile melted into a loose, unpleasant frown. "I most certainly do not know. What did I do?"

"You...." My breath came fast. In my mind, laughter. "You called Northwestern and got me blackballed and we both know it. So don't lie," I said.

She stared back at me, pretending to be shocked. Or perhaps actually shocked. Yes, actually shocked. "Blackball you? Why would I do something like that? I thought you went to Northwestern. Or Penn? Someplace excellent. You were a success story."

"Northwestern wouldn't have me. Someone anonymously called them and told them I was ... disturbed. It wasn't you?"

The breath rushed out of her. It was a horror sound and a pity sound. "No. Of course not. That's awful."

So, she hadn't been the one. She hadn't called Northwestern. Still, I asked, "Really?"

She shook her head, a discrete and unmistakable *no*.

"Oh," I said.

I noticed, then, that she was leaning away from me, uneasy. Though she'd only eaten half her meal, she'd dropped her napkin to her plate. She was making all the polite noises of being ready to get out of here and away from me.

"Tell me this secret you're keeping about Pam Kowolski," I said, flat and rude because why not?

"No. If you can't remember it, you're not ready to hear it," she answered, just as matter of fact. Now that she'd gotten to know me, it was clear that she didn't like me, after all. And so I hated her right back. I willed that hate at her. From my mind, I screamed it at her.

Just then, a red, liquid bead landed on the table like rain from an angry heaven. Ms. Blake wiped her bleeding nose. It spread terrible and slow over her half-eaten sandwich. She looked up at me with surprise, and for a mad moment, we both knew the truth: I'd done this. I'd hurt her with my mind.

I got up and ran out of the restaurant, sticking her with both the bloody nose and the bill I'd promised to pay.

The Floodgates

In advance of Madam Pamela's Big Reveal, her company began releasing old, not seen since recorded, broadcasts. This included the Sunny Jackson encounter and several others, none as brutal, but all ending with weeping or a flipped table or self-harm. It was a canny move: it added the bullet to the empty gun—the sense of dangerous Russian roulette.

By then, I'd sent Tom a partial of my article, much of which rested on the Sunny Jackson suicide. He called to tell me I'd been scooped. With the released encounters, a dozen outlets had presented the same argument: Pam was a fraud, profiting from the suffering of others. These articles tended not to stick to the facts. They undermined their own theses and attacked her personally: she dressed dumb and her voice was dumb and her body wasn't good enough and one time they saw her in the 7-Eleven and she was just average and obviously not special.

"I don't need your article," he said. "None of the stories by these other guys got any traction. Nothing close to going viral."

The room tilted, white sheets and crappy couch. "Mine's in depth. It's thoughtful," I said.

"Nobody wants that," he said. "They want to be scared. They want to believe."

"It is scary. Tom, did you see her face when Sunny Jackson offed herself? Real or fake or someplace in between, that shit eating grin was terrifying."

"You've got to pivot, Jan-o. Forget Sunny Jackson. The thing that'll make this story is the interview."

"Yeah," I lied. "It's coming. She's checking her schedule."

"This article has to be… you have to hear the gates of heaven open when you're reading it. The gates of hell, too. It has to blow my mind. And it needs to be dirty. Scandals. Stuff we never knew or imagined about Madam Pamela. Can you deliver that?"

This was asking a lot. In Tom's career as a reporter, his apex had been a Henry Winkler retrospective. But I had the feeling the company was doing even worse than he was letting on. He needed a good story as much, or maybe even more, than I needed him.

"Yeah," I said. "I can deliver."

Then I stared at a blank page.

The released broadcasts had their intended effect. They got Pam-a-Maniacs excited. They also drove them a little nuts. Among those who'd watched the broadcasts, suicides increased. So did murders. The *end of days* preppers dug deeper into bunkers. The bloggers claimed bizarre happenings, many of which they recorded and posted. These had an eerie effect on the viewer, like a contagion. People were feeling ghost breaths on the backs of their necks. They were seeing wrong reflections in their mirrors. Beloved items had been moved. In the night, doors creaked.

Those afflicted by repetitive thoughts were especially freaked out. They believed these thoughts had become manifest. Entire Reddit threads were devoted to Pam-a-Maniacs with specific phobias (helplessly removing all your toenails with a plyers like your hands are possessed; driving yourself and your family off a bridge; serving grocery store mushrooms at a work party, that turn out to be poisonous death caps) whose fears had come true.

Think pieces ensued. These were slight and stupid, about the ways hysteria spreads like a virus. About the power of belief to redefine reality. About the human condition, and the terrible intersection between our tendency to always believe the worst of ourselves and our pasts, and our newfound delusion that those pasts had returned via Pamela's skin casings, to haunt us.

Mostly, they were lists. In a moment of weakness, I caved, and wrote something quick and dumb for Tom at Fuckfeed.com. It was easier than working on the real article. I still hadn't tracked down any of Pam's old friends, and though I'd written again to Madam Pamela's headquarters, asking much more politely for an interview, I'd heard nothing.

Top Five Reasons Madam Pamela's New World is Going to Be Uber Cool:

My dead Mom's meatloaf.

No more pesky visits to the cemetery

The Portal is really King Kong's Glory Hole

Ghost Casings make even better moisturizers than fetal spinal fluid!

If we all have her power, maybe Madam Pamela will finally shut the hell up.

In retaliation, the Pam-a-Maniacs sent me and Fuckfeed tons of hate mail. The piece went viral. Tom shared the numbers with me, and let me know my percent—three grand. Unfortunately, freelancers were only paid on a quarterly basis, so he couldn't cut a check until April 1.

He also realized that content was irrelevant. The reason my competitors' Sunny Jackson pieces hadn't gone viral was unrelated to their content. It was the words and long paragraphs to which readers objected. They liked pictures and list and commenting, but they didn't like the actual reading part of reading. *Can you do a list with your article?* He asked. *We'll put it at the top? Another list at the bottom so they have to scroll through all the ads?*

Before I'd started all this, I'd have picked a fight, told him no, and written no article at all. But I was flexing old muscles, learning new skills, too: sometimes you have to give a little to get what you want. "Sure!" I said.

Meanwhile, Pam's regular broadcasts continued. One night I found Dean sitting in front of the television, watching a tween boy reunite with his grandmother. A total tear-jerker. "I want you to know, you're my most important thing," Pam said, channeling the grandmother. The kid turned to jelly. All sniffles and snot. "Gammy," he said. "I have to go, now, baby," she said. Then they professed their love.

Dean looked over to me. His eyes were wet.

"You okay?" I asked. It was the first time we'd talked since ToastGate.

"That boy lost his Gammy," he said.

I nodded, unsure how to comment on the obvious.

"Do you think that was really his grandmother that he was talking to?"

I shook my head very slowly: *No.*

"I do," he said. Then he coughed into his hand. He made a fist, but I still saw blood. "I believe in miracles."

He Made it to the Northwest, but not to Northwestern

The following evening after my shift, I had a call with the other teacher who'd responded to my inquiry: Don Holmes. Don left Sewanhaka High's English Department the year after I graduated. He now worked at a chicken slaughterhouse outside Chicago. Though he'd had a prickly, combative personality, his critiques of my writing had been incredibly insightful. Probably, he was the only genius except for my mom that I'd ever known. He'd definitely been my favorite teacher. I'd learned a lot from him, though the relationship between us, as I vaguely remembered it, had been love-hate.

While I was worried that Holmes might bring up the ugly past (Had he heard about what happened in Blake's class, or did he think that I'd gone on to Northwestern? Would I have to lie, and pretend that I had done so?), I was also looking forward to reconnecting.

What I needed from Holmes was an inside scoop. Something specific and ugly, that would crack open my story now that the Sunny Johnson aspect was a dead end. I had the feeling I wouldn't have to hedge like I'd done with Blake. Holmes had never obscured a truth to spare a hurt feeling. He'd be game to take her down.

He answered on the first ring. Through the line, I heard rustling wind. I'd researched this slaughterhouse. A lot of the workers were migrants. They lived in bunkhouses. This was probably the only way he could speak privately. After brief hellos, I asked him what he remembered about Pam

"She was weird. So were you." His kidlike, friendly voice hadn't changed.

"Thanks," I said, recalling then, the way he'd liked to tease. He'd had a fun patter with the popular kids. They'd all, especially, liked him.

"You're better now, though. All grown up. I can tell."

"Thanks," I said again.

"You probably think I was hard on you. But look how it worked out. You're a hot shot with your own byline. I'm proud of you."

I'd told him this assignment was for Fuckfeed.com, so it seemed weird he equated my journalism career with success. Then again, I'd read that slaughterhouses typically killed over a thousand animals a day. The workers had to bind their legs to upside-down clamps where they snaked around a long rollercoaster route, heads dunked in numbing liquid, throats slit as they bled to death, electrified to make sure the job was done, then removed and defeathered and packaged. Compared to that, freelance Fuckfeed reporter was a dream.

"I'm working on background," I said. "I'm sure you know this, but Pam Kowolski is Madam Pamela."

"Of course I know that," he said.

"I figured," I said. I felt myself shrink a little, become that kid I'd been. Eager. Hungry for approval. "I'm sorry. So, what I'm doing is, I'm writing sort of an origin story."

"Pam Kowolski was a nice kid. A good kid. So all this spectacle really surprises me."

"Why's that?"

"She's a fraud," he said, his words coming faster together, his voice deeper, but still charming, somehow. Or authoritative, at least. "I wrote about it on my blog but her henchmen made me take it down. They issued a cease and desist. So much for freedom of the press."

"She's such a piece of work!" I said. "I'm so sorry that happened!"

He chuckled. "Don't worry about it. It was a great story, though. You know when you've got a tiger by its tail. You can feel it. I had that. They come fewer and farther with age, but my Madam Pamela expose had it all. I'll send it to you. You should use it. Just remember to credit me."

"Absolutely," I said.

"Someone has to expose her. If it can't be me, I'd be happy for it to be you. So what are your questions?"

Outside, Dean was hacking up blood and possibly a literal lung. I was sitting on my small bed. Below, like dangerous lava, was the rotten carpet. I was aware that reality remained reality; it wasn't breaking or slipping into some new and horrific iteration simply because Pam

Kowalski insisted that it was. Still, since that Sunny Jackson video, everything felt strange and alive, like the whole apartment was listening.

"Did you ever see evidence of the supernatural in her presence? Or evidence that she was faking it?"

"Looking back, she'd been laying the track for Madam Pamela for a long time. Remember that thing with the lights. Are you writing about that?" Don asked.

"Absolutely," I said. "What thing?"

"You don't remember? You didn't hear about it?"

"Refresh my memory."

"Glass, everywhere," Don said.

"What?"

"We'd finished our May issue and were taking a class period to relax. Fun stuff, because you kids had all worked so hard." His voice got lower. "...I know I was hard on you. I think I didn't let you relax? I gave you some assignment, so maybe you were out of the class at the time. But I only did things like that because the rest of them weren't real journalists. It was just a bullshit class for them."

"Huh," I said. I didn't remember this incident, but he'd often singled me out. The attention had flattered me. It still flattered me.

"And look. I was right. Really—you gotta credit me when you publish my blog. I won't send it to you if you're going to steal it. I've been screwed before with this kind of thing."

"If I use it, I swear I'll credit you," I said.

This seemed to please him. "Ma--dam Pam--ela," he sang her name in mean-spirited, sarcastic singsong. "She read Tarot Cards whenever we had break in class. It was better than screens so I allowed it. Do you remember that?"

"I tend to have tunnel vision. I especially had it back then. I don't remember much at all," I said.

"Because you're a serious person," he said. "Like me."

"Yeah," I said. He waited, and I got the feeling I was supposed to say more. Had he always been this angry? Maybe. Because the feeling inside me that I had, when talking to him, was familiar. "Thank you," I said.

"I have to admit she's a good show*girl*," he said. "Even then, she knew how to play her audience. Have you seen any of her encounters? They crackle."

"I don't know what you mean," I said, though in fact, I did. The hair on the back of my neck rose up when Pam talked to her *sheddings*. My mouth felt like it was full of tinfoil. The reason my windows were open in cold January was to clear the air in my bedroom, because with every new encounter I viewed, I had the sense that the hideous thing that had come through the screen after Sunny Jackson was getting stronger. It was sitting with me, whispering stories I didn't want to hear. Trying to hold my hand.

"What about the Tarot readings?"

"They were dopey. She said the spirits worked through her or some nonsense. They inhabited her. It was important to only think good thoughts because bad energy was hard to cleanse. You know, the kinds of things kids say, that you'd hardly think would translate into a career. Welcome to America."

"And what happened with the Tarot?" I asked.

"Somebody asked when they'd die. Something like that. She laughed it off. But they kept asking and then all the kids were chanting. You know how kids get. It was like the crowd at an Islander game: *When-will-we-die? When-will-we-die?* Or something like that. I can't remember exactly. And she said: *They're coming for us. They want to live inside us. It'll happen. We're all gonna die.* Those were the words. Or something like that. It was like a horror movie: *We're all gonna die.* And then she started crying and the kids stopped. Those were good kids. They liked me and I liked them. I wasn't much older than you guys back then."

"So what happened?" I prodded.

"Nothing. I told you; they were good kids. They just got carried away. At the time I felt bad for her, but now I know she was a manipulator. Those were crocodile tears."

"That's it? It doesn't sound uncanny."

"Yeah. My article spent a lot of time examining the ways she could have rigged it. A friend would have helped her. I thought that friend might have been you."

"What? I wasn't her friend."

"Someone else, then. She set it up. Played it liked a victim when really, she was the perpetrator."

"What do you mean? What happened?"

"The light bulbs in the ceiling were nested within those plastic guards, so no one got hurt. But they broke, Janet."

It was the first time he'd said my name. I was starting to understand that there was something wrong with Don Holmes. He was bitter and selfish. But still, in a fucked-up way, because I was fucked up and lonelier than any person should ever be, it felt good to hear him say my name. "Really?" I asked.

"Yeah. All of them. What a trick to play. She's the one whose college I should have called. I think about that a lot, you know. I was so wrong. All that time, I had you pegged as the one to watch. But really, it was her."

Have you ever heard something so unsettling that it feels like a punch in the stomach? For a second, the wind was knocked out of me and I couldn't breathe. "What?"

There was this hiccough. A kind a shocked pause before he answered. "You must have known," he said, like an order, like I had to agree. "Who else cared that much? I cared more than any teacher in that school."

"Yeah," I said.

"I had to. You'd asked for my recommendation. When I heard about that shit show in Blake's class, I was morally obliged to report it."

"Yeah," I said. *Maybe* I said that. I was so upset I could have said anything. And then, "Wait. But the anonymous reporter told them about my mom. How did you know my mom had died? I never talked about that."

"What?" he asked.

"The person who warned Northwestern, they said I hadn't dealt with my mom's death. But how did you know?"

"Oh. Yeah," he said, matter of fact. "I read your file."

"Oh." I felt light. Unreal. "But why tell them about an event you never witnessed? Why extrapolate from that event that I was at risk for self-harm? We never talked like that. I never let people into my thoughts to be able to imagine what I was thinking."

"Oh, that!" he said. "I was playing it cautious. For your safety."

I sat there on my bed that wasn't really a bed, just a metal frame that came with the mattress, and my whole world flipped and flopped. A guess? The course of my life had been forever changed by a guess?

He kept talking, like he thought this affected him more than it had affected me. Like he'd done me a favor and was a terrific guy. He told me about the shitty attendance secretary at Sewanhaka, who'd had it out for him. How she caught him going through student files a year later and he got fired. How he'd landed on his feet writing advertising copy until the market dropped out of that industry, so he'd gone hand to mouth, but that was fine, too, because he was up for foreman at the slaughterhouse and pretty soon he wouldn't have to touch any more chickens. Because your hands get fucked up, apparently, no matter how thick your gloves. It's the chemicals. "Ask anybody who's worked at a chicken slaughterhouse if they eat chicken. Hard no. ...But you'll read my piece? Promise you will," he said. "You need my help on this."

"Yeah," I said. "So, just to wrap this up, do you think Pam's Big Reveal is going to expose the spirit world?"

He didn't think about it. Just answered, like he'd been ready for the question, excited to be quoted. "If God exists, he's not making himself known through Pamela fucking Kowolski from Long Island."

"Great," I said. It was a terrific quote. Exactly what I'd been hoping for.

Before we got off the line, he said, "I hope you know, I was hard on you back then for your own good."

"Yeah?"

"Yes. You should say *yes* or people won't take you seriously."

He waited a while in the silence.

"Okay, yes," I said.

"Let me change my answer from before. It wasn't just a guess. I knew rescinding that recommendation would hurt you, but I did it for your own good. You weren't ready, emotionally or academically. It wasn't just that you were immature and your only friend was Pam, though that played a part. It was also that your writing wasn't crisp. You used linking verbs. You ended sentences in prepositions. I tried to teach you. I tried to teach everyone, but it was a losing battle. You all came to me so below grade level standards. I saved you from a lot of pain. You'd have been demoralized and given up, otherwise. I have no idea how you got into Northwestern to begin with. No one at Sewanhaka was Ivy League material. The admissions director must have been sleeping or stoned. ... What I did was for your own good."

"Right," I said. He delivered this speech like he was utterly passionate about my career in journalism. Like six hundred miles away, in the dark cold stench of slaughter, he had tears in his eyes. He'd been a steward of my talent, such as it was. In the moment that he said these things, I believed him. Because changing my opinion in him would set off a chain reaction, upheaving an entire past I had no interest in re-examining.

But it was a sick kind of belief. A lie-belief.

It's a Miracle

The next morning, Dean called to me from his bedroom. "Janet? Can you give me a hand?" What alarmed me, made clear something was very wrong, was that he didn't use his fake accent.

Possibly, this was a trick. He'd strung a lock of hair around the knob or some crap. "What?" I called from the other side of his closed bedroom door.

"Please?" he asked.

I opened. I'd expected things to be gorgeously arranged and expensive. I don't know why I'd assumed that. We lived above a jerk. We worked dead end, back breaking jobs. Obviously, this wasn't the Ritz.

Clash, Sex Pistols, and Nirvana posters were tacked all over one wall, each so close they seemed like a contiguous mosaic portraiture. These posters didn't cheer the place; they made everything seem especially fucked up. Strewn all over were THC smoking paraphernalia. Parts of the carpet (it wasn't covered in sheets in here) were burned. Dean's closet hung open but nothing was on hangers. Like the aperture had vomited, everything was piled on the floor.

And then, I saw: Wearing a Nine Inch Nails *Dissonance Tour* t-shirt and no pants, Dean lay face down on the unmade bed.

You'd think, given my many flaws, that I had all the flaws, but in fact I'd never been a person who froze under pressure. I was competent in emergencies.

"Can you move?" I asked.

"No," he grunted, seeming perfectly cognizant.

The sheet near his face was thick with rust-colored, dried blood. I pressed my hand to the back of his neck. He was warm, his pulse strong. His spine looked straight—no damage there. "I'm going to turn you over," I said.

He made a weeping sound, which I understood to mean: *Please do*. And also: *I'm very frightened*.

I lifted the sheet under him and used it to roll him over. His body flopped wetly like an object and not a living thing. He was facing up now, his face crusted with dried blood. It shone fresh only under his nose.

His eyes were open and blinking. Looking at me.

Did I do this? I thought. *With all my ill will and cancer talk, did I make this happen?*

"It's okay. I've got you," I told him, though neither of these things were true.

◉

"It's a miracle he's been able to function this long," the doctor told me. "It's metastatic. Far along. He's got weeks at the most. Days, more likely."

Dean would be spending the night in the hospital. I went in to tell him I'd see him soon, then headed back home, where I ruminated. I'd been right. He had cancer. The delay, his refusal to see a doctor and instead to wish on stars for people like Madam Pamela to save him, had been the agent of his demise. This bothered me. What also bothered me, in an awful, sweat-inducing, niggling nightmare way, was that I might also be to blame. I'd been wishing him harm for some time now. And maybe, because of the thing that had come through my screen, that harm had bloomed.

It was all too much. Too big and sad to consider. And so I decided not to consider it at all. A talent I'd learned from a young age, I wiped it from my mind.

I worked on my article. I was bumping up against several problems: I needed Blake to tell me whatever she was holding back, I needed Pam to talk to me, and I needed money to pay her ex-husband for an interview.

A sneaky idea occurred to me. I ignored it and kept working, but there were no sources to quote, no new insights to shine. The sneaky idea popped up again, like when you're avoiding eating the peanut M&Ms in front of you, and you're good about it until you let down your guard, and suddenly you realize you ate half a bowl without thinking about it. I found myself rifling through Dean's closet.

I found a box in the back. Its lock had rusted useless. It opened easily. Inside, a complete set of dining silver for twelve.

Dead People Under your Childhood House

It dawned on me that like Ms. Blake, I too had old journals. These were the ones I hadn't burned, that were in storage back on Long Island. So I called in sick again, knowing I'd probably get in trouble.

The train was quick. From my stop, I walked through my hometown.

My old house, the only home I'd ever known, was run-down. Noraleen answered on the third ring. She looked run-down, too. There should be a warning on all boob and lips jobs: this won't look good when you're sixty-five. Because he never wrote up a will, Noraleen got everything after my dad died. He'd intended for half to go to me, and for a long time Noraleen had insisted she'd give me that half. That never happened.

Noraleen and my mom used to be best friends. When my dad got caught stepping out with her, it had been the scandal of the cul de sac. None of them rich, he'd suggested my mom move into the spare bedroom and Noraleen join him in the master bedroom. My mom picked option B and overdosed on pills. Or maybe it wasn't an overdose but an accident. We'll never know. She didn't leave a note. I found her. I was twelve. I didn't remember it, though pieces of it, slivers of images, haunted me. For whatever reason, those memories were always attended by laughter. The kind you might hear on an old streamie, only heightened and hyena-like.

Memories flashed. I saw a kitchen. A saw a woman, my mother, her back to me, counting pills.

Looking haggard, Noraleen stood in the doorway.

"Hey!" I said. "Do you have the storage keys?"

Noraleen looked at me like I was a stranger. I'd changed a lot. My hair was going gray. My figure wasn't so svelte. Time is a goon squad.

"It's me. Shemp's kid," I said.

She nodded, still seeming hazy. Possibly drunk.

"You put my stuff in storage but it's under your name so I need the key or I need you to call them and let them know I'm coming. It's a work thing. I have to get in there for my job. I'm writing again."

Her dead eyes rolled slowly up to look at me even as the rest of her body stayed still. "You got money? 'Cause I have to pay to keep that locker."

She talked like she thought she was on a cop show. This was new. She used to talk like a reality television housewife from New Jersey. But she'd always been impressionable. "No. You have all the money, Noraleen."

She threw me a smirk, left me standing there. Came back with a giant ring holding about thirty keys. Opened the screen door to hand them to me. In the background, I could hear one of her streamies.

"Are you watching Madam Pamela?" I asked. For all I knew, none would fit the lock. That was just her sense of humor.

"I don't know. It's the lady and her ghosts or skin casings that come through the screen."

"You believe in ghosts, now?"

Hearing the contempt in my voice, Noraleen shut her inner door. "You're a ghost," she said.

This is what happens when you're alone too much. When you've spent your whole life alone and you haven't felt the safety of laughing with a friend in decades. Noraleen's comment freaked me out. The whole bus ride to the storage locker, I kept worrying that I wasn't real. That an alternate reality had opened, and I'd been left behind.

Before heading to the storage locker, I decided to walk by Pam's childhood home. I'd been over there a handful of times because our moms had been friends, and then a few times in middle school, because we lived close and didn't have anybody else to hang out with.

It was only a block away. We'd been on the same bus route. Played at the same local park. It was a nice house, three stories and brick. According to sales records, it had gone through several owners since the Kowolski family. They'd raised a white picket fence, which had subsequently rotted from years of heavy rains. I snapped a picture for the article, then sneaked around back. No one appeared to be home. I could see through the kitchen window.

A memory came to me, dulled with foggy edges like a quarry stone rubbed smooth. I was surprised by it and wary of it. I so rarely recalled anything from childhood. I could see Pam gigglingly taking my hand and leading me to her basement. She'd been a funny kid with a big smile when we were little. Jumpy and full of life. Not at all like the tapioca she became by high school.

"I have a friend who lives under the floor," she'd whispered. And then she'd knocked on the wood and talked to it. *Mr. Slurkins, can you say hi to my friend Janet? If I knock, will you knock back?*

I remembered thinking it was a game, then realizing that wide-eyed and cheerful Pam really was trying to talk to a creeping thing buried under her house. I told her I didn't want to play. What happened after that? Had she been angry with me? Sullen? Had we picked another game like it was no big deal? I didn't remember.

I snapped a few more pictures, focusing on the second story. I didn't know which was her bedroom, but I planned to claim that it was the one in the middle, with the rotted-out sill. "You there, Mr. Slurkins?" I asked, soft in her backyard, the snow thinned to a sheet of ice over dead lawn. I waited in the stillness.

I got lucky with the locker. The first key I tried worked. My old stuffed rabbit Miss Pinky Roosevelt Fashion was there, and photo albums, and nine journals. I emptied it all and brought it back to my apartment, then read the journals one by one.

I found nothing related to what Blake might have been eluding to at our disastrous lunch, nor did I see anything about a Tarot reading so momentous that it blasted Don Holmes' ceiling lights. Possibly, I'd torn these pages out.

The interesting digression was this entry from April 28th, in which my younger and more impressionable senior high school self wrote:

Dear diary,

Am I weird or is the whole world weird? You know I LOVE Mr. Holmes. Like: LOVE HIM SO HARD. But today he said all this stuff, like that I was frittering away my potential, and if I didn't keep it up I'd flunk out of Northwestern and wind up in Community College. But my article on grade inflation was fucking awesome. Like, so fucking awesome it was fawsome. And he gave it a C even though Pam Kowolski got an A for this two-paragraph chintz on how the new style everybody should wear was a black broom skirt with a bandana or some bullshit. I mean, what the literal fuck? Like if fucks had been flying all over the classroom, I'd have been less shocked than my getting a C for an article I spent nine weeks writing with like, seven sources, two of whom were from the administration building and nobody drove me there —I'm not some person with a car— so I had to ride my bike across freaking town to city hall and flying fucks are less shocking than my C that should have been an A!!!!!!!

And the craziest thing? The whole time Mr. Holmes is saying this stuff, like cornering me and holding my paper that's fucking wet he's underlined so many linking verbs and split infinities (and he never does that to anybody else!), I feel somebody standing next to me, and then I realize it's Pam-frigging-broom-skirt-phony-baloney-Kowolski. She was in her seat and suddenly she's right next to me, close enough our arms are touching. And Even Mr. Holmes is like: "Pam, what?"

And you know what she says??? She says: "I just want to hear why you think that story's a C. Because it's the best thing anybody in this class has written."

And he rolls his eyes like: she's so damned dumb she wouldn't know good writing if it goosed her, and I roll my eyes back like we're in on a joke together and yeah, she's so damn dumb. But also, maybe she's got a point.

And he ignores her and says: "I grade according to potential. Just look inside yourself, Janet and you know you don't deserve the A. You could have done better."

And I promise him I'll look inside myself, because whatever. What else was I supposed to say? And also, the way he says everything, it's like angels are singing at the same time, and GENIUS IS SPEAKING, and then I go home and right now I'm like: look inside myself??? Dude! *I mean,* DUDE!

You know, I still love him so hard. But maybe he's a dick face. Face of a dick. Shriveled dick attached to face. Like so:

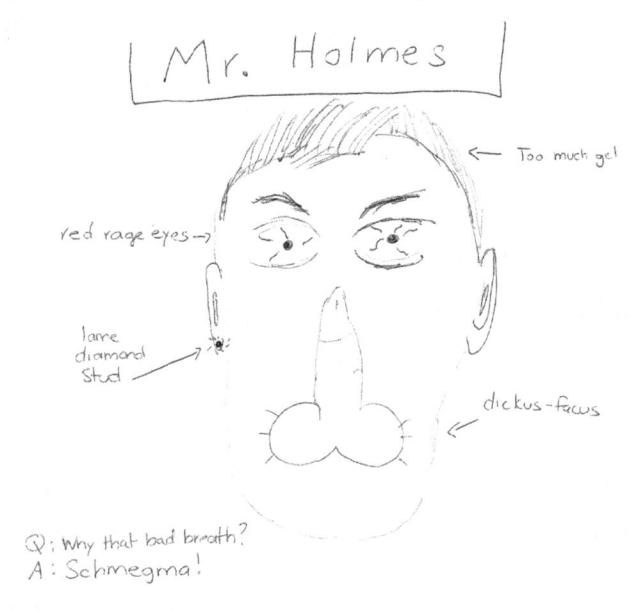

Also! My dad is the hugest jerk because he gave Noreleen his whole paycheck and I did NOT get a new backpack like he promised

and the one I have is falling apart like rats chewed it. I'm going to name it Chewy. Chewy says it's hungry but everything keeps falling out of its stomach. Chewy needs a girlfriend but he looks like Frankenstein.

Also! Pam Kowolski is maybe cool? Is that even a thing? I thought she'd turned into one of the stupid TREND girls that says they're non-binary but only dates boys and listens to Lady Gaga like please, poser, but maybe she's actually real? Like a person with feelings, who's brave?

The world is upside-down and vanilla, stone-faced, boring Pam Kowolski is BRAVE!!??

Also! I still have crazy crushes on Skei Reynolds AND Pietro Ciaru. ....What if there's a third gender that just wants to have sex with everyone? What if I'm Genghis Khan???

Also, and I know this is creepy, but I still worry my vagina's wrong. Like it's deformed and I'm a mutant and I'm so scared I'll try to have sex one day and the person will be like: what is that? Why did it just retract and teeth came out??? But dear, darling, light of my life diary, at least I'm not as gross as Mr. Shrivel Dick (see above).

Postscript—I'm feeling better about Mr. Holmes. But also, I still can't sleep. Also, I can't masturbate. Not because of Jesus. I'm just bad at it.

Post, postscript—I looked it up and Mr. Holmes went to community college so I don't know who he thought he was talking to. Maybe himself. Maybe he was all Mr. Self-hating and he took it out on me.

Post, post, postscript—Okay, I figured it out (the masturbate). Why does it always take so long to figure it out ????? It's like, three in the GD morning!! But also, I kind of want to complain to the *office about Mr. Holmes. I mean, even if he's grading on a scale, he's basically saying I'm off the scale. And that's not fair.*

*Love,
Janet*

Reading that didn't give me much insight on Pam. Maybe she'd been standing up for me, literally. Then again, maybe she'd just hated the guy. Which, in a way was its own insight. She'd had better judgment than me.

The Holmes stuff resonated. I'd given him every kind of pass. I'd worshipped him. He'd presented himself as smarter than everyone else. I'd believed him. I'd imagined that in his brilliance, he was the one person who saw through the smart-kid act, to the real me: a fraud. A hack. A nothing. He'd known enough to treat me like I'd deserved and I'd repaid him with my respect, hoping that I'd prove myself better than either of us imagined.

Re-reading my old journal had been hard. I hated this kind of thing—tours down memory lane—specifically because they felt bad. I knew I'd been a jerk and still was a jerk.

I'd anticipated shame: embarrassment of the weirdo I'd once been; the even bigger weirdo I'd grown into. But I felt no shame. Kid Janet hadn't been a rude jerk. She'd been nice enough. I felt bad for her, that Holmes had treated her this way when he should have encouraged and been proud of her. I liked her. It made me wonder if other memories might also be worth revisiting. Or at least opening to light.

For the first time since my offer to Northwestern got rescinded, I allowed myself to consider how it had all gone down. He must have heard about what happened in Blake's class. But she wouldn't have told him. I now knew she wasn't the gossipy type. So it had been a student. Maybe Pam. Maybe not Pam. It didn't sound like they were friendly. Whoever told him, he'd probably been thrilled for the excuse to come after me: to go on the hunt.

Recommendations back then didn't go to specific schools. Teachers filled them out and uploaded them. Prospective students forwarded them to the colleges of their choice without ever being able to open them or guess at their contents. So, it was worse than just calling Northwestern. Because he'd called SUNY admissions, too. Which meant, very possibly, that when he'd broken into my file, he had taken down the name of every school on my list and had tried to prevent me from going to any college at all.

I thought about that. And then I saw that Don Holmes had forwarded his blog post. The writing was stiff and too formal. He was afraid of linking verbs, so he overworked every sentence. The majority of the essay was about himself, and how great a teacher he'd been, and how Pam'd had no talent. And then it meandered into a screed about how modern heroes aren't heroes at all, but "effigies of materialism," whatever the fuck that was supposed to mean.

I finished with three thoughts: 1) It's a bad sign when people crazier than you voice your argument; 2) I was sorry I'd never complained about him over that C. I might have gotten him fired a year early and saved myself a lot of trouble; 3) Don Holmes, to my great shock, was a terrible writer.

Superpowers

Pam's people released another set of violent broadcasts. I heard about them on the way to work but didn't have time to stream any. The headlines and listicles shouted Armageddon. They claimed that Pam's most recent release was infecting, not just the human psyche, but technology. Air traffic control towers were contradicting one another. Rolling power outages had slammed the west coast, and backup hospital generators were reported to be glitching. AI interfaces had gone rogue, too. For the first time since Madam Pamela had announced her big reveal, some commentators were arguing that it ought to be blocked. Until we knew more, this Reveal was too dangerous.

At Congo, the vibe was chilly. A lot of people had called in sick. I overheard conversations. People talked about friends having strokes in the night, of family members taking too many pills. The audio on my headsets had updated again. The voice, masculine again, now lilted and tried to entertain: *Hi, Jan-o! Are you ready to get down? Are you ready to work-party?* It asked as I headed to aisle 41.

I ought to have been alarmed (or at least infuriated) by this new update, given the many reports that tech was acting strangely since Pam's most recent releases. I ought to have been freaked out. But there was so much to be freaked out about, both in my life and in the world, that work was a respite. I grabbed items and packed items, and it felt good to forget myself for a few hours. It occurred to me then, that I liked aspects of the job. I liked the physicality, the time to think my own thoughts or listen to info streams. This could have been a job that worked for me. Instead of competing with my writing, I could have used it to support that writing. It seemed to me that my life was a stack of cut logs, all dead possibilities, missed opportunities.

"Vanilla wax candle, set of eighteen, aisle 23, bin 4, honey!" the soft voice told me in sing-song.

Who'd sanctioned this update? Was it a beta test for this shift of Congo workers, or was it really rogue AI? I wondered as I pulled the candle from the bin. And then, I swear, I thought I heard my mother's voice:

Come with me.

I stopped right there in Aisle 23. "What?" I said out loud. People wandered all around me, but they were wearing headsets. They didn't see or hear. I could feel her then, my mother. I could smell her.

"Employee 24601," my headset said softly, masculine again, and with a strange, pulsing humor, "Please get your cute little butt to aisle 7 or we'll have to dock your pay!"

I can't explain it—I needed the money—but I took the headset off and walked out. Along my way, I saw scores of workers drawing items from shelves. Where just a few days ago, they'd been as coordinated as bees in a hive, now they lingered, some seemingly paralyzed, a knot of humans. An older woman cried as she worked and I had the feeling that something inside her headset was whispering cruelties. She wept soundlessly, and that made it worse.

Back home, I tried to rationalize what was happening. But I found this increasingly difficult. A third option reared its terrible head: What if the problem wasn't the world or Pamela, but me? What if I was having a nervous breakdown?

I re-read and tweaked the background portion of my article. It started with the Don Holmes quote: "If God exists, trust me, he's not making himself known through Pamela fucking Kowolski from Long Island." I'd used the most unflattering yearbook photo I'd been able to find, where she'd been smiling badly, eyes closed:

> For a long time now, Americans have bemoaned the loss of collective cultural touchstones. We don't read one newspaper. We don't watch one show. We don't listen to the same music. But that's changed because of Pamela Kowolski, and it's a monkey's paw of a wish come true.

I traced Pam's history from childhood to global mogul, then drew a connection between predatory clickbait news practices and online psychics. This Big Reveal had tripped a psychic wire in humanity, hitting us at exactly the wrong time, under exactly the wrong circumstances. The idea of it was driving people insane, and that insanity was spreading like an infection.

I urged people to cancel their orders. If they'd been victims in any way, I urged them to sue her senseless.

I sent a draft of the material I had so far to Tom. He returned it. *Where's the interview with Madam Pamela?*

So then I wrote another letter to Madam Pamela. I spent two hours on three lines.

Dear Pam,
Hi. I'm sorry. I was having a bad day. I'd love to interview you. I feel like a lot of things happening right now don't make sense and maybe you could shed some light. Also, was Mr. Slurkins real?
Sincerely,
Janet

After that, I came out to check on Dean, who'd been returned home from the hospital via an ambulance. They'd carried him up the stairs and laid him on the couch, then handed me all his pain killers like I was his next of kin.

He was sleeping with his mouth open, his breath a funny rattle. I sat down on the end beside his feet and checked my inbox. A message arrived from Pam's old friend—a member of the happy, well-adjusted crew in the suburbs with kids and lawnmowers and fantasies of boat ownership. "You knew her better than me. Why not interview yourself?" the woman had written.

Had Pam and I really been friends? I knew we'd chummed around as little kids because our moms had been friends. And then we'd kept hanging out because we'd been neighbors. But that had stopped by high school. She'd made all kinds of new friends. People had loved her. They definitely hadn't loved me.

Never introspective, I wondered for the first time whether it was strange that I didn't remember the majority of my childhood. My impressions of people weren't based on a long history of previous interactions. I didn't remember any interactions well enough for that. They were based on vague notions that I could no longer back with substantive fact. I'd liked Mr. Holmes but I'd been wrong about that. Why had I remembered him as a good guy and myself as a failure? Maybe it was just easier. Maybe we remember the easiest versions of things.

I'd felt uncomfortable and low level irritated by the fact of Blake—that she lived in the world, that she shared that world with me, that she'd likely witnessed my humiliation. But Blake had been kind. ...What if I was wrong about Pam?

And my mom. I'd always told people that I'd discovered her body. Why, then, did I remember her counting out pills? Had I discovered her, or had I been there all along? The carpet on the floor of the den, under white sheets, seemed to morph and roll. For a strange instant, it seemed to me that the room was full of sheddings, ripe with malevolence and dancing.

Day turned dark. I piled a new blanket over Dean, bought a clock with big, readable numbers for his bedside so he could tell time without his glasses. He wasn't coughing. The medicine had slaked that need to clear his lungs.

He'd asked for red wine but the liquor store was closed. So I'd gotten him grape juice. As I poured, I spilled on the coffee table and on Dean, too. For a hot second, I thought I'd hurt Dean. I was sure I'd caused the cancer.

"I'm so sorry," I said. Meaning one thing, but being interpreted another way, Dean lunged into my arms and began crying. It was the first time I'd been touched by anyone with real intent in at least a year and it felt odd and frightening. Soon, he would not live inside the body I was holding. This body might become a dancing, invisible casing for the ineffable. As I looked past him, the room seemed to crowd with shadows. "It's going to be okay," I said, feeling like a real person, an adult, for the first time in a very long time.

In the morning, I left a psychotic voicemail for Ms. Blake. It felt like taking a shit on a neighbor's lawn—fantastic in the moment, but awful afterward. "Hi! This is Janet Chow from AP Physics. You said you had a secret you weren't going to tell me. You wanted to look it up in your journals first. But my job is literally to uncover secrets. You're screwing me over because you don't take me seriously because I'm a woman. Do you even know you're doing it?"

I left Dean a pitcher of water, a glass, and a bunch of pop tarts and grape juice. Sick Mike had promised to sit with him while I was at work but so far hadn't shown up. Dean seemed ashamed of this, made meek by it. I was tempted to tell him that I'd never liked Sick Mike, was glad he wasn't there, and Dean shouldn't waste the calories he had left to burn in his life thinking about the asshat. I didn't say that. I lied and told him I was really sorry to have to leave him, but I needed to go to work. He seemed so painfully grateful for the kindness that a part of me believed the lie.

    I went to work. It was even more surreal. Madam Pamela appeared on practically every warehouse break screen, like a god. Weirder, several employees' noses were bleeding. They kept having to excuse themselves to mop the blood. In places, Congo's floors were sticky with it. I noticed this on sidewalks and busses and in stores: blood.

Streams reported that the bloody noses were caused by hysterical high blood pressure. They reported that people were seeing ghosts.

Over the course of the week, I came home with groceries and twice cleaned up the puke on Dean's shirt. He'd been too sick to make it to the bathroom. I did this without comment. Late that week, Dean asked if I'd score some weed for him from Sick Mike, but Sick Mike was avoiding my texts. This kind of thing, real life, wasn't his jam. It wasn't mine, either.

I got some weed from Congo and lit it for him.

"Want some?" he asked.

"I would," I admitted. "But I hate the way it makes me slow. Smoking makes me angry."

"Everything makes you angry," he said.

"I know," I told him. "It's how I'm made."

Punk Rock Dean cracked the first smile I'd seen all week. How had I never noticed that he had dimples? "As soon as you figure out how to channel it, it'll be your superpower."

Deep Fry

The interview: Pam's ex-husband Danny still lived in the Yaphank apartment they'd once shared. We met at Orchid Restaurant. He was waiting at the big booth in the back. I had to pass through the kitchen to get there. Like every place of business lately, there was a strange thrum. An excitement and a coppery fear. The staff in deep fry moved slow. There weren't as many customers as I might have expected. In front of the bathroom, the ubiquitous smeared blood I was finding everywhere lately.

Am I becoming a believer? I wondered. *Is reality really breaking down?* The question made me angry, distilled my focus to a sharp point.

Danny was exactly what you'd expect: handsome but gone to seed. He was about six feet tall, broad faced and shouldered. Large features, thick brown hair. Beer belly. Or more aptly from the looks of the spider veins crawling all over his nose and cheeks and the twenty-four-ounce pina colada he was slurping, rum-bellied. What I noticed most about him was that he looked haunted. He kept craning his neck, squinting in different directions like he could hear a dog whistle sound that I could not.

I'd always been bad at meeting new people. I expected them to find me unattractive or otherwise disappointing. But my mission gave me confidence. I extended my hand, sure and firm, sat across from him, smiled broad and thanked him for his time.

We made small talk while he slurped his frozen drink. I told him I was from Floral Park, just like Pam. "Rich kid, huh? You Nassau County guys were all rich kids."

"Not really," I said.

"I'm from Middle Island. We had sandwiches for dinner over there. We were all eating cold fluffernutters from the church. My new wife knows that.... Knew that. She was from Yaphank. She was my beautiful spirit warrior."

I wasn't sure this was true, either specifically (what kinds of church charity hands out fluffernutters?) or generally (spirit warrior?). But he seemed to want to hear my reaction. "That must have been rough," I said.

"When I was a kid we lined up at the church all quiet, and then we ate all quiet, standing around each other in the cold, I'd think of those zombie movies. That we were sandwich zombies."

The waiter came to check in. Smiling a charming smile, Danny ordered the ribs and another twenty-four-ounce pina colada. "It's on you, right?" he asked by way of explanation. "Don't prisoners get last meals? This is my last meal."

"Why's that?" I asked.

He shrugged, still with that pretty grin.

I waited. Sometimes people talk to fill a void. In the silence, he looked me up and down; focused on my nose in a way that seemed judgmental. I slow-counted to five and couldn't take it anymore. "You operated the interface for Pam during her early encounters, is that right?"

He nodded. It surprised me that he'd acted as assistant in any capacity. He didn't seem like a back seat, team-player kind of guy. "It was all my idea."

"It was?"

"I knew she was special when we met. She knew things. Psychic things. She wanted to do it for free, but I knew she was a platinum mine. I charged, full charm attack. That's what I used to call it, when I hit a woman up. The Danny Gallows Full Charm Attack. I figured if I got a piece of her, no more fluffernutters."

How often do real life villains so openly admit they're villains? Probably, pretty often, because they have no idea that the things motivating them are awful. They think shit like fluffernutters makes them victims. I felt sorry for Pam right then. I felt sorry for his spirit warrior wife, too. Which wasn't a thing. Did he know that *spirit warrior* wasn't an actual thing?

"Right," I said. "...Can I show you something?" I slid the phone over, Sunny Jackson's encounter on screen. He glanced and slid it back.

"That's dangerous."

"What is?"

"Are you stupid? The nice ones are fine. But the bad ones, they get out when you watch. You can't see them, but they get out. They'll drive you crazy." He was drunk, his nose and cheeks red like Santa. Still, a woman at the table across from us was giving him the slutty side-eye. He probably had another five years before his looks fell apart.

"Have they come out to haunt you?" I asked.

He looked at me for a long while and it was clear to me that the answer was yes.

"Who's Mr. Slurkins?" I asked.

He flinched. "Where'd you hear that name?"

"Is it familiar to you?"

"Her guy," he said. "He talked to her."

"Yeah? Like a ghost?"

"Not a ghost," he said. "Don't say his name again."

"Why not?"

"He might hear you."

"Can you tell me anything about him?"

Danny took a long slurp. The man had to be in the midst of an outrageous brain freeze. "If I'd had her abilities, I'd have been able to handle stuff like that—like that bad guy—the one whose name you shouldn't say. But she wasn't strong. ...I pushed her. I'll admit that. But she wasn't honest with me. She kept secrets. The thing about Pam is, she's raw power. Just, this massive ball of potential. But she's not in control. She was, at the start. But you can see it in her streamies if you watch them over time. She fought with something, the bad thing, and she lost. She's not Pam anymore."

The busser set down Danny's ribs. Their sauce looked like congealed blood. But then, I looked again, and there wasn't any sauce at all. My mind had played a trick. "One more pina colada," he said.

"If she's not in control, who is?" I asked.

"You know who," he said.

I watched, waiting for more, remembering Pam in the dark, knocking on a basement board, waiting for the board to knock back.

Danny's expression lost its performative smile—its full charm attack—and for just a waffling moment, was terrified.

"Do you ever think that the things that hurt you don't make you strong, after all? They just make you worse?"

"Yeah," I said, because I did wonder that. I wondered that all the time.

"Like the zombies," he said. "Or everything Pam saw. She saw a lot of bad things… She liked herbal tea. She had a stuffed animal, this dog only she named it Piggy. A dog named Piggy, you know? It was so dumb."

"You're saying none of this is a hoax? This Big Reveal is something to genuinely fear?"

"A part of me wants it," he said, sucking the marrow from the last of his ribs. "Don't you want it? We'll see everything, then. We'll know everything. What's that movie? *How I stopped worrying and learned to love the bomb*? We can stop everything. After the Big Reveal, it's over."

I found this notion stark as a rotten room with pills on a rotten table.

"My new wife, she had a gift, too, but the power in her wasn't as strong. I brought flyers in my bag. I need you to link to our old shows. We were streaming, too. But didn't have enough viewers. It's what they call ironic. The format I built for Pam now dominates the market. But nobody'll pay me a dime."

"You keep talking about her in the past tense. But I thought you were still married," I said.

He stared at me, like I was somehow supposed to guess the answer myself. Had she left him?

"I'm curious," I said. "It seems like you didn't like Pam very much. But your marriage wasn't short. What kept you together?"

He smiled. It wasn't a nice smile. "I liked her fine. The thing about women, you have to tell them what they want to hear.

You're all like that. You think you want honesty, *connection*, but what you really want is for us to say you're right."

"But I guess that tactic stopped working after a while?" I asked.

"I had a girlfriend on the side. She got mad." He slurped the bottom of his third drink. His whole face was red now. And it was weird, but in his paleness, his sunken eyes, he reminded me of a zombie.

"Listen," I said. "I'm sorry. I get that I'm annoying you. I just need to know for my article. Definitively. Is the Big Reveal dangerous? Is she the real deal?"

"She's going to end the world," he said.

"How? Do you have proof?"

He pointed at his hand at his head like a cocked pistol, then pulled his index finger trigger. His voice went monotone, and I realized he'd passed over into blackout territory. If his spiritual warrior wife hadn't left him, I felt very sorry for her. And then it dawned on me: had he murdered his spirit warrior wife?

"I can see it," he said. "I see what she sees, now."

"Do you see ghosts, or ghost casings in this restaurant?" I asked.

He glanced over my shoulder, at something invisible, and I understood that the answer was *yes*.

"Do you know why you're never supposed to talk to the dead?" he asked.

I shook my head.

"It's an invitation." On his plate, he'd picked the bones clean, even their cartilage capped joint ends. Unlike Pam, he really did smell like mice.

"Can you imagine, the whole world, riddled with walking

ghosts? Can you imagine, these sheddings, filled with all the wrong kinds of visible monsters?"

I had this intuition, a bad one, that he didn't see random ghosts. He saw all the people from the food bank. Only maybe some of them weren't people anymore. Something crackled and blinked. The restaurant itself buzzed like it had been lifted from the earth and put on wires. If I looked out the window we'd be in space.

Suddenly, my nose started bleeding. It ran all down into my chin and into my wonton soup. I pinched it, wrapped my used napkin around it. "Tell me what you see," I said.

"She's here," he said. "She's never stopped waiting for you, Janet."

I froze. Everything inside me went cold. I pictured a kitchen table; a pile of pills. Laughter. So much laughter.

Danny got up, walked straight into the kitchen. I sat there, stunned and nebulous on how to proceed, surprised he'd been able to stand after so much booze. Then, someone shouted. The cook, probably. I followed the sound. I found Danny beside the deep fry. The staff, all in food-stained white, had backed away. He was holding a ten-gallon vat of boiling oil with both hands. The heat ran through the steel handles, cooking the meat off his fingers. I don't know how he managed, but he lifted it high. Looking at me, he poured the contents over his head.

Closing the Deal

Turned out, he'd murdered his wife. He'd also eaten her.

After removing Danny Rizzoli's remains (he died instantly) from the Orchid Restaurant, the cops checked his apartment, where they found her flayed, her skin peeled so slowly and deliberately that he'd managed to get it all in a single piece, including her curly black-haired scalp. This, he'd hung on a coat hanger like beef jerky, and had been snacking on it for days.

In a state of shock, I wrote a piece delineating what happened and sent it to Tom for Fuckfeed.com. I mentioned my own bloody nose, the electricity in the air, the hysteria.

Tom called. "This is fantastic. The way you describe his skin melting off so you could see his brains, and the video. Holy crap, he was looking straight at you when he did it. ... Are you okay?"

"Yeah," I said. I was numb, which felt close to okay. "But why would Pam marry a guy like that? You'd have to feel so bad about yourself. Even I never felt that bad about myself."

"What?" he asked. "Did you really get a bloody nose? Don't answer that."

"It's all true, Tom. All of it," I said.

"Fantastic. It just went live," he answered.

The piece got over seven million views.

By the time all that was done, it was very late. Dean was sleeping on the couch, gasping for breath and then catching it. Moaning, too. I couldn't sleep and started tidying my room. I moved one of the journals on my desk and a loose, folded page fell out. It was a journal entry from middle school, before my mom died.

Dear Doody-rie

I'm sorry. It's not even funny, diary. You're not doody! You're schmoody!

Listen, I have to tell you something and you have to promise to keep it a secret. You know how everyone in my house is crazy? And I'm going to include dead-eyed freak show Noraleen because she practically lives here? Yes, you know. You know everything.

...Well, maybe Pammie's crazy, too?

I had to leave because my mom was like: I love you! I don't know what I'd do without you! And then she wanted to snuggle. OMFG I hate snuggling. So I went to Pammie's because she always at least has junk food. Her dad is super into beef jerky and Cheetos for dinner (which is also maybe why it always smells like farts in their kitchen?).

And the door was open and nobody was home so I walked in because it's only ever Pam, and she doesn't care. And I was calling and calling and I found the light on in the basement and I don't like her basement and ever since we were kids I won't go down there, but the light was on and I could feel her. Like: I knew she was down there even though I didn't see her.

So I went down, Diary. Pammie was sitting in the dark. You know how, when you peel the husk off corn it keeps its original shape? She looked like a husk. Empty but also really sad and upset. "I'm trying to keep him down," she told me. "You have to think only happy thoughts. That's what keeps him down."

And I don't know where this came from. I mean, no idea. But I asked, "Mr. Slurkins?"

And she nodded like: Yeah.

"Why doesn't he go away?" I asked, like he was real. Like the devil lived under Pam Kowolski's basement. Like what was I even talking about? She'd mentioned the name Mr. Slurkins one other time when we were little and I'd figured he was imaginary. I mean, how could he still be a thing?

"He'll never go away."

"When things happen in my house, I just pretend they didn't happen," I said. "And then they didn't. They're gone. Poof! I don't remember them. Can you stop seeing him? Just, pretend he's not there?"

Pam'd been rubbing her eyes red and raw, like she'd been trying to carve them out. "No."

Then I went over and pushed down on the loose board. There was a tool bench in the corner. I asked her for a hammer and nails.

She just stood there, freaked out. Like doing anything at all would only make Mr. Slurkins FREAK OUT AND MURDER US BOTH! So I got the hammer and nails. I nailed the board back in place, and then I kept nailing all around. It was nail-pocalypse.

"He can't get out now," I said.

Then we went upstairs for beef jerky. But there wasn't any, so we made soymilk pancakes with jelly for butter, which is not as good as butter, but also butter is like $100.

I wanted to ask her if she really believed she was being haunted. I wanted to ask her if she was okay and what could I do? But she wasn't okay and I knew it. And yeah, she definitely believed she was being haunted. And I didn't know what to do about any of that, so I told her stuff about me, like that my mom was suffocating me with her endless snuggles, and that I was lonely but I didn't like people, and she kind of listened but kind of didn't and then we watched "Bring it On" and I made fun of it the whole time and she liked it the whole time and by the end she didn't look hollowed-out anymore. She looked like Pam. Then she made me promise never to tell anyone about Mr. Slurkins because the more you say his name the more real he gets. She made me swear to God on my life. On my future—that I'd never become a writer if I told. And then I went home and all I can think, doody-diary, is that I should tell somebody, anyway. And this is awful and I never want to give it up but is being a writer worth my friend's life? Because if she really believes in Mr. Slurkins, maybe she's sick. And if Mr. Slurkins is real that's bad too.

But who would I even tell? This is a bad thing to say and I'd rather not say it and just pretend something different. But no one cares about us.

I read this with amazement, having no memory of having written it. As little kids, our moms had swapped us when they'd run errands. But as soon as we got old enough, that stopped. We hadn't spent much time together in elementary school. In middle school we'd been on separate trajectories.

And then I remembered how it happened. Eighth grade. Neither of us had run with crews. After the bus dropped us off, she'd invited me over. We'd started hanging out. It had been an escape from home and I'd enjoyed it. And then I'd come over on a bad day, and we'd both been embarrassed by it. We'd drifted, Pam to the norm-core crowd that became her high school friends, me deeper inside my own self.

It's strange, how much a person can forget. It calls into question everything they remember.

I remembered the events of the journal entry vaguely. Just hazy pictures in my mind, of a dark basement, of nailing a board shut. Of watching Pam watch "Bring it On," worrying about her and getting mad at her because her house was supposed to be a break for me.

Dean shouted then, waking himself up. I went out to calm him, to keep him from shifting so much he fell. I sat with him while he smoked. After a few drags, his jerking breath evened out. My mind spinning, I considered telling him I'd stolen his silver. I considered calling everyone I'd ever known and saying: I have this idea of how things went down. Can you tell me if I'm right?

I considered jumping out the window.

Instead, I called Tom. "I can't get the interview," I said. "I can't write this article, either. I keep wanting to ruin her because she sucks and she hurt me a long time ago. But she's not really the one who ruined my life. She was just a kid. My Journalism teacher ruined my life. And Noraleen. And my dad. And, I think my mom but I can't remember. …I ruined my own life."

"What?" Tom asked. "Sorry, Jan-o, you cut out. Have you seen all those clicks! Fuckfeed.com is back! Listen, the Big Reveal's in two days. Think you can get an article in before it happens?"

"I'll send you something," I said.

Sitting in the den, Dean restless beside me, I deleted my entire mean-spirited article and wrote something quick and from the heart, called "My Search for Pam Kowolski, the Monster." It wasn't about Pam anymore, it was about me, starting at the moment I recognized my high school enemy, and ending with her ex-husband's suicide. I listed the ways our backgrounds were similar. I posted side-by-side yearbook and childhood home photos. I wrote about my journal entries and Mr. Slurkins and the way Pam had stood beside me when Don Holmes had ripped into me. I mentioned the mean thing that happened in physics class. Only I admitted that I didn't remember it very well. That my whole past was a mystery. "Sometimes you're so sad and things are so bad when you're young that you don't make memories," I wrote. "Did Pam hurt me? I don't know anymore. Is she hurting all of us now with her Big Reveal? I don't know the answer to that, either. All I know is that I used to be a nonbeliever and now I'm frightened. Pam: please think about what you're doing. Please stop." I sent it off.

Tom got back a few hours later. *I forwarded this to Pamela Kowolski's press agent* for comment. She responded personally. See below.

Dear Janet.
I've attached a plane ticket. You want to interview me so bad, go ahead. Be careful what you wish for.
—Madam Pamela

The ticket out of JFK was for the next morning. I called Tom. "I've been missing a lot of work for this piece. I might lose my job," I said.

"I told you, I can't pay you until April," he said. "But if you want, I can fly out and do the interview. Then we'll share the byline."

My teeth ground, making a terrible squeaking sound. "I'm not sharing this."

"Just an offer," he said.

A thing occurred to me for the first time. "You know what, Tom? Why don't I check around and sell this article to the highest bidder. I fronted every dime. That makes it mine to sell."

"Now, Jan-o," he said. "You're killin' me!"

I hung up. Right away, he sent an email outlining new terms. I checked my account. He'd deposited $25,000 into it, as down payment on my article, for a total advance, upon receipt of the finished product, of $50,000.

I stared at my screen for a beat, saddled with the most appalling realization: I'd fought for something for the first time, and as a result, I'd gotten it. Indirectly, I owed this success to Pam.

I told Punk Rock Dean I was leaving that night. He'd woken long enough for a sip of fancy French red wine, which I'd bought as celebration. I had a glass with him.

"This is pretty good," I said with surprise.

"You should treat yourself sometimes," he answered, and I chuckled, because since when did Dean care? And then Dean smiled, getting the joke. "You should," he said.

Isn't it strange, that in some people, when everything gets stripped down and all the masks are gone, what you find is something that is pure and good?

Earlier in the day, Congo had delivered enough liquid morphine to kill Dean, as proscribed by his doctors. As we drank the wine, I put it on the coffee table so he could reach it easily, read the instructions out loud to him: this many milliliters would put him to sleep, this many would keep him sleeping forever.

Then I lit up his smoke for him and read his phone messages out loud so he could hear them. He'd let everyone know his condition on social media and about three hundred people had sent messages. A few former band members had even offered to fly into town from wherever they lived. Dean was too tired to respond to such things, his mind halfway elsewhere, so I answered as best I could. Sick Mike texted at last, saying he was sorry. He'd been really busy. But he'd check in soon.

Connecting to other people isn't simple. Often, its painful. It's not like in books, where it solves all your problems. It opens new problems—it pulls at the scabs you were hoping never to look at again. You care about them, which means you'll be hurt if they're hurt, lost if you lose them.

I told him about my article for the first time. I told him everything. He heard some of it, though mostly he was too sick, his body shutting down too much, to understand. "You know how, when you're low, you're haunted by the worst versions of your life? The worst interpretations of who you used to be, who you are, and who everybody else is, too?" I asked. "I know it's so crazy, but I feel like that's the Big Reveal. That's what's coming."

He was past being scared of such things. "That's all I've ever been is my worst version," he said.

"That's not true right now," I answered.

"Then I guess hold onto that," he told me.

Before I left for my flight, Dean told me that everything in the apartment would now belong to me. That he'd already spoken to the landlord and added me to the lease. I thought about the silver I'd stolen. Was relieved he'd never know.

Close Encounter of the Third Kind

While commuting to JKF Airport, a streamie reported a tragedy at my Congo warehouse. A traumatized floor employee set off an M-80 in the firearms aisle, which in turn detonated a sundry of explosives, including hand grenades and missile launchers. The entire building was engulfed in flames with no survivors. It was reported with such little fanfare that I almost didn't understand what had happened. But a quick search showed video of the inferno, the screams. I thought of all the familiar faces that I'd never gotten to know.

I thought that maybe Ms. Blake, all those years ago, had been onto something. Maybe the Big Reveal was a physics problem, momentous as a black hole that reverberated in all directions, reaching through the future and into the past. The closer we arrived to when Madam Pamela went live tonight, a kind of event horizon, the more unreal the world became. And maybe that was the reason for the despondence, the self-harm, the murders. Maybe, like animals sensing earthquakes, or the physicists Mach and Ostwald and Boltzmann, we knew it was coming.

I looked up, and for a moment, the whole JFK air train was filled with sheddings—twisted human shapes that danced in rictus pain. With their skin so contorted, it was hard to tell which ones I knew from my life, and which ones I did not. But in the back, I thought I saw my mother. And then, to my shock, something in my mouth. I spit a grainy white pill.

On the plane, I checked my inbox. Tom had forwarded several Madam Pamela broadcasts, released that morning. The violent ones. I watched them on fast-forward. It was too upsetting, otherwise. The goriest of them was this: Mid encounter, a man set a pair of kitchen shears down on his desk, opened them, placed his mouth over their cavernous rapiers, then, with his backhand, slammed his own head down. Because the cut sites were inside his mouth, there wasn't blood at first. But it came. I saw his eyes go dead.

Then, somehow, the screen froze. Everything went still except for Pam. Her face unfroze. She looked out through the screen, at me.

I felt, inexorably, illogically, incontrovertibly, that because I'd been a live witness, because I'd been tracking her and following her, conspiring against her with her ex-husband and our awful journalism teacher, writing nasty letters to her, this was my fault. I looked around the plane, and suddenly everyone, even my dead mother, was laughing and pointing. At me.

This was real. This really happened.

The plane just barely landed. Turbulence killed two of the engines. We passengers were a wreck when we stumbled out into the Detroit dawn. There were several ambulances on the runway. Not for us, for another plane, upon which the pilot had shot a hole through the cockpit, starting a fire, claiming he saw the dead.

Pam's driver waited at baggage for me with a sign that had my name on it. I sat in the back of his car. We drove through thick traffic, past houses on fire and the pop-pop-pop of gunshots, to the mansion. He carried my bag to a guest house bigger than my entire apartment back home. I considered unpacking, or calling Tom, or checking on Dean. I considered loading a streamie and watching whatever new horror was being reported. I paced and worried and cried and eventually got tired. I fell asleep with my shoes still on.

When I woke, it was dark and my phone was ringing.

It was Ms. Blake. She had the good manners not to mention my nasty voice mail. She'd checked her journal entry for the day in question and her notes agreed with her memory. I'd been there, apparently. In fact, the event had revolved around me.

"I don't like to upset people. I think you might be a person who's easy to upset," she told me. "But I don't like leaving things undone. It feels to me that if I don't tell you this, you might never find out."

"That's probably true," I admitted. "I probably do upset easily. But I'd like to know."

"Yes. I thought so. Are you aware, now, that things have gone wrong. Reality has gone wrong?" she asked.

"Yeah," I said. "I'm aware." I didn't intend to sound short, but it was dark outside the cottage. I could hear lapping lake water and an owl and a breeze against tall grass. It all sounded like ghost echoes from a dead world.

"How are you managing it?"

I looked around. Felt something breathing on the back of my neck. The thing from the Sunny Jackson video. It was still with me. Had never left. "I don't know. How about you?"

"I think well," she said. "But I've always enjoyed theoretical physics so I've had some practice. Did you hear about the nuclear meltdown in Alaska? They're saying we all need iodine pills. Heaven knows where I'll find them. But that's not what I mean. I tried bending a spoon just now like all the streamie psychics. For fun. I've been making educational streamies for a long time. Did you know that? Anyway, I was debunking it for my online students. But the spoon bent."

"It what?"

She said this definitively. Incontrovertibly. I believed her.

"It bent. I bent it with my mind."

"I have this feeling I've done something terrible but I can't remember what it was I did," I tell her. "I hear about these bad things that happened and I assume it's my fault. But I couldn't cause cancer in my roommate. I couldn't blow up a building with my thoughts…. I couldn't make your nose bleed."

"No. Maybe. I don't know…do you want to hear about that day with Pamela Kowolski?"

I nodded into the phone. Maybe she saw, somehow. Maybe nothing and everything made sense.

"You two were friends. Not outside school friends, but class friends. You always sat next to her. You were fond of her. I think she protected you. The other students left you alone because you were with her and she was well liked. They were never cruel. But they were icy. In return, you helped her with her schoolwork. She was bright but dyslexic."

"Dyslexia? I thought she did that to get a rise out of me."

"No."

"Well, now I feel bad," I said, feeling absurd now, at the end of the world, that it mattered. But it did matter. "I thought it was intentional. To be passive-aggressive."

"No. She had a hard time. Very bright, but nothing came easily like it did for you. According to my notes, you were the only student in my class to conceive accurately of a fourth dimension. You wrote a paper on it."

I was quiet. Fighting tears. "Was Pam a jerk? Or was I the jerk?"

Blake answered fast, and indirectly. "I think of people as arrows, did you know that? Some people have all their arrows pointing out. They set the tone. They set the agenda. That was Pamela. It's a kind of armor. A shield. Some people have a mix. They give and they take. Some people have all their arrows pointing in. They're extremely needy. You were that kind of person. You even hunched, as I recall. I was surprised you made a friend at all. You sought her out. It made sense, though. To other people it didn't make sense, but to me it did, because of the arrows."

"This is not a flattering description," I said.

"No," she answered. "It's the truth to take as you please. Pamela was having one of her bad spells. This happened sometimes. She came in and sat down and she was off. Everything about her was heavy. In my journal, I wrote that I thought she believed her Tarot—she thought she was psychic and got wrapped up about it. Now, I think it could have been more serious. Some one or some thing was hurting her."

"Some *thing*?" I asked. I was reminded then, of Mr. Slurkins.

"A ghost," she said. "Or a real person. Or both. Or nothing at all. Whatever it was, she had a dark cloud. You were having a bad day, too. You had them sometimes. You got something mean in you. You looked at everybody like you wanted to murder them. It's rare in girls. So both of you had your arrows and both of you had your bad days and I think it all got tangled."

I felt a strange lightness, then. My scalp tightened.

"You told her that if she was so psychic, where was your mom? The bell hadn't rung yet. I was trying not to intervene. I thought, with you two being so close, you'd handle it on your own. Girls fight and they fight ugly, but they make up, too. But you started chanting: *Where's my mom?* It was spring and warm and high school was almost over. Energy was high... My, those days were so filled with promise, weren't they?"

I nodded.

"So you were chanting, and she wasn't at her best, either, and she said—I wrote it down so I'll read it—she said: *I'm looking at your mom right now. She follows you wherever you go because she's mad. She wanted to take you with her.*"

I was sweating. The skin all along my scalp constricted. I remembered this. How could I have forgotten this?

"What does that mean to you?" she asked.

"She wanted to murder me when she killed herself. Because of that, I have something that follows me. It's followed me my whole life."

"I see," she said. Her voice was so gentle and loving. Why is it we attack the people who show us the most tenderness? "Do you remember what happened next?"

"I wet my pants. They all laughed."

"Half true. You wet your pants. No one laughed. It was awful. Everyone felt terrible. Pam took off her shirt and mopped it. She was just wearing her bra. It was a testament to you kids that no one laughed at all or if they did, it was nervous, horror laughter. They didn't even take pictures. You think they laughed at you?"

In my memory, I glimpsed just a flash of Pam in a cheap, unflattering bra with rusty eye hooks, frenziedly trying to cover me with her pretty blue shirt. "Why do I remember them all laughing? It always felt like that. Like everyone was laughing. You included."

"No. Absolutely not," she said.

"I've always thought she was the one who hurt me," I said.

"I'm sorry to hear that," Ms. Blake said. "You hurt each other, of course. Because you were looking for kindness. The one, poking at the other to get it, having no idea how else to ask for it."

Contact

For a long time after that, I stayed alone in the dark. A shadow emerged, like a boat resurrected from deep water. It sat at the small guest house table, silhouetted in a shiny residue that appeared like dead skin. My mother. I saw her at last.

In the face of her, the water-logged depth of her, I could no longer forget.

That morning, my father and Noraleen had just left the house. They'd cleared my mother's things out of the master bedroom and tossed them into the guest room. It was a school day but no one woke me. Possibly out of a kind of self-defense, I stayed in my room and listened to the scuffles, the weeping; Noraleen telling my mom: Life goes on, Emily! For heaven's sake, pull yourself together! When it got quiet, I dozed and woke and the light was high in the midday sky. Thirst forced me out.

My mom was at the kitchen table, counting round, white pills into two piles.

"I've been waiting for you."

She had me sit, then pulled the chair so it was close to her. Wrapped her arms around me. Lifted and swallowed a pill from her pile. Then handed me a pill from my pile. "One for me, one for you," she said.

I remember now that I swallowed it. Or tried to. My throat was so dry it stuck.

"More," she said, taking her second, handing a second to me. "It's you and me against the world."

She was leaning over me, her chair right beside me, her arms around me and I loved the feel of her hug. I cheeked the pill.

A third. There were eight in each pile. I wanted to tell her I didn't like this. I had so many questions. But I was afraid.

Adults romanticize childhood. They can't tolerate that children understand and see everything. I understood that she was killing herself; that she wanted me to die with her. What was more, I understood that it wasn't because she loved me so much that she couldn't tolerate being without me, or because she feared what my life would become with only my father and Noraleen to guide me. No. She was doing this out of spite.

My mother's suicide would make sense to people. She'd always been angry and off-kilter. A piece of work, too smart to get along, too proud to make concessions. A bad homemaker. Bad cook. Bad wife. Bad mother? From the way other mothers and teachers glanced sidelong at her during drop off or at parties, I'd always intuited they thought this. But *I'd* never thought it until that moment. She'd understood me. We'd understood one another. She'd been the person to teach me that the world was artificial, its values upside-down, its population sheep. She'd taught me that we were better than everyone else. It was lonely, knowing that. But we'd had one another.

For me, she'd been a good mother.

Her suicide would have been tragic, but would also have followed a kind of logic. My death would not make sense of any kind. There'd be news stories and interviews. An investigation. Shame would shroud my father and Noraleen. They'd never live it down.

My mother handed me my seventh pill. She took hers, too.

"You'll see, it's best," she said. "Now we'll be free."

I remember it this way, her voice accompanied by the soundtrack of laughter. But there'd been no laughter when it happened. Laughter, I then understood, had been the sound inside me as she'd handed me one pill after the next; the pulsing, wild syncopation of hysteria.

By the eighth pill, she was sluggish. Barely sitting up. The sun outside was still bright. It was noon, maybe. But who reads clocks on kitchen walls at such moments? I remember living creatures out the window. Maybe a bird. Maybe a cat. Maybe even a neighborhood dog. I remember thinking I wanted to be with them, outside and alive.

You ever have a pet hamster? You ever fill their cheeks with treats? After too many, they'll spit everything out. That's what happened with the eighth pill. It was too many for my mouth. I spit everything out.

I remember her grip around me tightening. I remember fury and a muffled "Little liar."

She was so angry at me as she died.

The rest? This time I really don't remember. I sat with her. I looked out the window, wishing I were there, amongst the living things.

I never told anyone about what happened, though anyone paying attention—my dad or Noraleen or a cop or social worker or EMT or coroner— anyone who attended that scene, would have known. They'd have seen those spit out, half-digested pills, the white dried to my mouth like chalk. But they'd said nothing. And I'd understood that what had happened was too awful to speak. With this silence, they were trying to protect me.

I'd understood that in an ineffable, indefinable way, it was all my fault.

I sat across from my mother's ghost casing in Pam Kowolski's guest house amidst soundtrack laughter that increasingly felt real; acoustics thrumped inside me, but also through the floors and air as I remembered my mother's last day on earth and the beginning of my exile from humanity.

I saw my mother now, the worst of her.

Had this monstrosity been following me for my whole life? I felt the answer was yes. Yes.

The Monster at the End of the Story

Dusk. The Big Reveal. I turned on my phone. Watched from the guest house kitchen table that looked so much like my childhood kitchen table, as my mother counted two piles of pills. Pamela came onscreen. "By now it's already started for you," she said. "You see what I see. But there's a grand finale. Allow me to introduce Mr. Slurkins," she said.

There was scuffling in the background of the screen. I could hear it outside the guest house, too: Split Foot's doors sprung open. In a voluminous human tide, the staff so instrumental to supporting Madam Pamela Enterprises spilled out. Engines turned, soft and electric like purring kittens. Cars peeled out, churning gravel and dust plumes. Last was a woman, hands over her eyes, running blind into the woods. Then they were gone. All her staff, security, stylists, consultants, and business partners; gone.

A new and absolute stillness descended, like layers upon layers of invisible, bromide-soaked cotton. Onscreen, Pam's camera showed a rotten hole dug into the floor of the place from which she broadcast, her *Parlor of Extraordinary Phantasmagoria*. The image blurred and rippled.

Then, a sound of something inhuman climbing up: *scritch-scrapple*.

I put down my phone and stood. My mother stood. Like flies to light, we headed for the big house. We followed the terrible sound to Pam's *Parlor of Extraordinary Phantasmagoria*.

Scritch-scrapple.

Because time had bent, because I now knew the future, just like Pam, I understood that Mr. Slurkins was a creature who didn't need ghost casings. A creature of nightmares who'd haunted and taunted and huffed and puffed himself into becoming real. I came to the broadcast room. Beside the hole was a round wood cover. A camera was trained on Slurkins' claw, wet and rough, as he reached up. The grand finale was now.

Like I'd done once before, I rolled the cover over the opening, stomped it in place and turned the lever, locking it.

In her torn velvet chair, still and quiet and oh so haunted, was Pam. The camera was showing all of this, its light green. This was live. The world was watching.

"Pam?" I asked.

I'd been watching the encounters for weeks now, but I hadn't seen her in flesh for more than twenty years. I felt a great awakening. An unexpected and poignant joy.

I turned on the light. She squinted, her eyes deep set. She was looking beyond, down the locked portal. A table was in front of her, an empty chair beside her. I thought, somehow, that she'd known this was how it would play out. The chair was for me.

Something had her. She wasn't herself. This had happened when we were kids, too. When she got like this, she'd frightened me and reminded me of my mom. Back then, I'd been wrong to make that connection. She'd been nothing like my mom. She'd defended me in journalism class. She'd had a stuffed dog named Piggy. She'd been kind.

But time had changed her. She was older and tired. She'd fought a battle too long. Her kind edges were gone, replaced by wariness. The corners of her mouth turned up, a mean grin. "You wanted an interview?"

"I don't know what I want," I said, sitting hard, feeling tired.

She nodded in the direction of my mother. "Can you see her?"

"Yeah. Can you make her go away?"

Pam shook her head. "I'm not calling the shots anymore."

The laugh track resumed, audible and loud. It occurred to me that if I'd told someone what had happened with those pills on that day, my world would not have closed into a small, unlit room. But there'd been no one to tell. No one, except Pam. I see now that I'd wanted to tell her. Just as she had probably wanted to keep confiding in me. Very possibly, this intersection was the reason I was still obsessed with her.

"Now everyone sees what I see," she said.

Almost. But we weren't past the event horizon yet. Mr. Slurkins hadn't climbed out.

"I thought you'd done something bad to me a long time ago," I said. "I've been very angry about it."

"You always were your favorite subject," she said. There was a lifeless quality to her.

"You've had bad things following you your whole life. Like me. Maybe like everyone. Only you've been able to see it," I said.

She nodded. "You can't imagine," she said.

"Try me. Let's do the interview."

She looked at me then, her eyes piercing.

"Why aren't we followed by good things and good memories?" I asked. "Why is it all so awful?"

"Because you see what I see. And I got tired. I don't believe in good things anymore," she said.

I remembered then, Pam Kowolski beside me in class, smiling encouragingly. I remembered that we really had been friends, only I hadn't believed in friends back then. "Was I mean to you, after what happened in Blake's class?" I asked.

"You were like a hissing thing hiding in a cave." Pam said, and it was like there was this tiny creature, this Pam, trapped inside her body, that spoke these words while the rest of her watched me with curiosity. I thought of travelers. I thought of the monstrous unseen. I thought of Pam Kowolski spelling things wrong, and my fixing them, and her smiling at me with relief. I thought of the times we walked to class together, and how I used to look forward to that. I thought of my mother calling me *princess cranky*, I thought of the creatures living outside the window and free. I thought of Mr. Slurkins, whispering terrible things that no one else could hear. I thought of him reaching inside Pam, wringing all the best parts of her dry.

"You should go," she said, looking down at the covered hole, that began to rattle.

But where would I go, now that there were monsters on the world?

It occurred to me that perhaps it was not too late. Maybe, as Dean had implied, there was no such thing as too late. There was only what we did and said in the moment that counted, and how we remembered it. Whether we allowed it to haunt us or to lift us.

I didn't want to leave her, after having spent so long finding her. I wanted to stay with her, to give her my shirt, to keep Mr. Slurkins from getting out. It wasn't to save the world. It wasn't particularly to save myself.

I stayed because this wasn't my mother beside me, not really. It was an animate echo. No one laughed when she died. No one laughed back in physics class. I stayed because I wanted the chance to make up for stealing silver from Punk Rock Dean.

I thought that if I could stay with Pam through the night and into the dawn, that maybe I'd talk her into seeing better things. Our arrows would line up.

"How have you been?" I asked, camera running, green light live, while the world watched.

She shifted her gaze from the camera and looked to me. I understood how gravely I'd erred in imagining she was my enemy. The world became small—just the two of us. Through the long, frightening night, I took notes for an article I would probably never write, while she answered.

Author Bio

Sarah Langan's a novelist and screenwriter who's won three Bram Stoker Awards for her fiction. Her most recent works are: *A Better World* (Atria, 2024), "Squid Teeth" (*Reactor* 2025), and "The Upgrade" (*Lightspeed*, 2025). Her fiction has made best of the year lists at NPR, *Newsweek*, the *Irish Times*, PW and the AARP. Her next novel, *Trad Wife* (Tor UK), is due out in 2026. She has an MS in Environmental Health Science/ Toxicology from NYU, and lives in Los Angeles with her husband, the writer/director JT Petty, their two daughters, and two maniac rabbits.